£2.49

C000094876

Grievous Love

LOVE BETRAYAL TRAGEDY

by

Alan Dawson

Grosvenor House
Publishing Limited

This book is published by
Grosvenor House Publishing Ltd
28-30 High Street, Guildford, Surrey, GU1 3HY.
www.grosvenorhousepublishing.co.uk

A CIP record for this book
is available from the British Library

ISBN 978-1-907652-41-7

*Dedicated
to the memory of my friend
Harry Cocks*

ONE

1826. The summer, which had been comfortably warm, began to give way to darkening nights, misty lowlands and burnished leaves as autumn approached. For Will and me the past three months had been busy. Every week during that time we had travelled around Surrey, and occasionally into the adjoining counties too. Every fair we had attended during the summer had its own rhythm and charm, which added to the excitement and made each a real adventure for me. But there was still a living to be made, and so our time from dawn to late was for the most part spent at our pitch at the fairs. Will loved to be there. He was quite the showman. Shouting out to passers by to come over to see the shoes and boots that he had made so carefully. By early evening each day we were both tired and hungry, and it was such a joy to leave the noise of the fairground behind and return to the tent that we pitched nearby.

My life now was one that others would not perhaps wish to follow. We were what folk called trampers, moving from place to place and living a nomadic life. It gave me a great sense of freedom. A great joy being in the open, unencumbered, together. But there were times when I thought what might have been. The sight of the ladies whom I had seen during the day, dressed so beautifully, carefree, laughing and happy, each on the arm of a fine looking gentleman, did make me wonder. But, then again.

It had not always been like this. Until my late teens I had lived with my parents in an altogether sleepy village in the county. Local people went about their business, tending their own smallholdings and looking after their livestock. Some worked on the several large estates in the area. We all lived for the most part quietly and peacefully. The village had a thriving market, which each week attracted hundreds, and then life was much more interesting and lively. The tavern, situated at the crossroads in the centre of the village, was always busy that day from first light. Even in the early hours of the next day it still disturbed our sleep.

My mother and father had always been honest and hardworking. Truly devout Catholics they had attended the local church every Sunday for years. My father was not born a local man. He had travelled down from the north about twenty years earlier, and had had the quick good fortune within days of his arrival to meet my grandfather John Akehurst, a lawyer and church elder. John had taken immediately to my father and had offered him work as a clerk in his practice in Leatherhead. That's how he came later to meet my mother. They were married in 1806 and I was born the following year.

*****

The local schoolhouse, which I attended, was just down the lane from our cottage in Bookham. I had enjoyed school from the very first day, and especially art and divinity studies. My teacher, Mrs Soper, had taught at the school for many years and was regarded highly by everyone in the village. It was she who encouraged my art and I recall many times sitting with her in the village as we tried to paint a picture of buildings there. In my final year at school I had quite a number of paintings that people said showed merit, and so when a fair came to our village that year they were shown at the art exhibition. That's how I first met Will.

Will, who at that time was still apprenticed to his father, was about four years older than me, and as he had been a traveller, some say a gypsy, all his life he hadn't had the same chance of an education as I had had. What he knew is what he had seen and heard. But he was without doubt a confident, amusing and assured young man, liked by everyone. I had noticed him first when we were watching the ploughing competition in the top fields. He was with a few of his friends and they were making quite a racket shouting at each of the competitors as they made their way carefully up and down the fields. It wasn't until later that day that I saw him again. This time he was at a pitch his father had where they were mending riding boots. He had simply looked up and given me a gentle smile. It was the first time I remember feeling self conscious, but it didn't stop me staying there.

'Can you mend these? ' I had asked, pointing to my boots, which after three years constant wear had seen better times.

'Maybe...what's your name?'

'Mary. Mary Ayres.'

'I'm Will. When I've finished these in a minute or two, can I buy you an ice cream?'

And that 's how we started. That was three years ago now.

I finished my schooling that year and although I didn't see Will again after the village fair, we did meet up by chance when he came back at Christmas time alone to sell in the local taverns the boots he had made. By then he had started to work for himself. He spoke about the fairs that he had visited since we had first met, and suggested that I ought to sell my pictures at them too. It set me thinking. And so in the following year when the fair was again in the village I took a pitch, hung the paintings that I had prepared over the winter, and realised then that this was how I could make a life for myself.

*****

It was often said of my grandfather John Akehurst that fortune frowned on him. Born in neighbouring county Sussex he lived there until his parents moved to Surrey when he was ten years old. His father, a merchant trading in animal feeds, was a successful and much respected businessman in the local community. That is until the early and unexpected death of his wife. Her death had a profound and severely disturbing effect on him, and although people were at first sympathetic to his situation, his heavy drinking and bad temper eventually became a burden to all, and he was shunned. His business in time suffered too and the family were soon a pitiful sight.

My grandfather, then in his early twenties, was at that time in training as a legal clerk at a practice near Dorking. By all accounts he was a diligent and hardworking man, such that his principal was able after five years to make him senior clerk. His life was essentially uneventful for several years, with most of his time being devoted to his work and community matters. But the sudden closure of the practice changed all that. No one really knew the circumstances. Some said that fraudulent use of clients' funds was involved. But then again no prosecution had followed. It was this event that prompted him to set up his own practice in nearby Leatherhead the following year.

Single until thirty he met and married within five months a neighbour, who had been widowed two years earlier. But their happiness was short lived, she dying in childbirth the next year. For five years after her death he had lived a fairly solitary existence, employing only a live in nanny to care for their young daughter, my mother, until one day he decided that he also needed a housekeeper. It was then that he employed an elegant looking lady named Elizabeth Haines, well known in the village both for her devotion to others, as well as for her excellent cooking.

There was talk in the village soon after she joined the household that the relationship between the two was close. It was even mooted that the reason the nanny had been dismissed in the following year was that she had become aware of that and had started to speak openly of it to her friends. Whatever the background and the arrangements in that household, what is a fact is that my grandfather and his housekeeper lived in the same house together for over thirty years without, it was said, ever a harsh word. Now in their retirement he tended the vegetable beds proudly set out by him, while she attended to the flowers in Bookham church, a short stroll from their cottage.

I have always been close to my grandfather and have tried to keep in touch with him, but this was not always easy with the travelling I was doing to make a living at the fairs. But I had written to him in late summer and promised to pass by when I was in the area that October. As that day got nearer my excitement was fairly uncontained.

*****

John Akehurst eased himself from his chair. His knees cracked and pain sheered through his left side. He made no sound. He had got used to being what he described as decrepit. He made his way over to the hearth, warmed himself for a short time against the open fire that by now was beginning to burn brightly. He turned to see Elizabeth come through from their front room. He smiled and she acknowledged that without saying a word.

'Well I'll be away now, ' he said. 'I have a meeting with Tom shortly. I'll see you around eleven I suppose.'

'Fine. Mind you don't get cold, the wind is strong today and it's fresher out there than it looks. I've put your jacket by the front door.'

As he stepped out he understood what Elizabeth had meant. He braced himself against the freshening air and started the short walk into the village. As he passed the butchers at the top of the main street he viewed a couple of men he did not recognise. He paused for a second, without wanting to catch their eye, but ensured that he had a measured look at them. They both were in the early twenties, dressed untidily as if they were off to work in the fields for the day, and he thought their manner seemed to him to show that they had interest in noting activity in the village. He thought no more of it, passing them without comment.

He entered the offices of Taylor and West down a short alley at the top of the main street. A young lady seated in the front room welcomed him politely, and as she did so Tom Taylor came through greeting him warmly.

'Good to see you. You're looking fit. How's the leg today?'

'Fine,' he said rather curtly not wishing to spend too long discussing his ailments. 'How's your family, Tom? – I heard that that daughter of yours is doing well at school.'

'Very well indeed, thank you. Anne's settling in well by all accounts. We both have high hopes for her.'

The two men had been friends for at least fifteen years, ever since Tom Taylor had settled in the village to join Sam West at his practice. Unfortunately Sam had passed away within two years and Tom had worked alone since that time. Their conversation then moved to a discussion about John's request to amend his Will. He was anxious to ensure that he had accounted properly for everything as he hadn't viewed his will for several years and some of his sentiments had changed. He wanted to ensure that Elizabeth would be well provided for, and to make adequate allowance for his daughter. He was conscious that hers had been a difficult life, not made the easier by a husband whom he had at one time thought a malingerer.

He read the amendments made to the document before signing it.

'What's the date Tom?'

'Thirteenth of October.'

The business concluded, the two friends then sat and enjoyed each others company talking about John's days in court and current legal issues, which interested them both. After about an hour John said his farewell, and made his way back on to the street.

On his way home he spoke only to a couple of acquaintances, whom he had met at church over the previous months, before walking across the main street and through the gate into the churchyard. He followed the path to the church's large wooden door, which was wide open. As he entered he met Father Bolland, a portly man with a kind face. They had become well acquainted with each other since his arrival in the parish three years earlier and they had often spent evenings since then playing chess and sharing a fine wine.

'Good morning, John. Wonderful morning isn't it. How's Elizabeth and the family?'

'Well, thanks.'

And with that curt reply he made his way to his seat at the front of the church. Kneeling he whispered his prayers, before rising, crossing himself, and walking slowly to the back of the church again, where the priest was busying himself rearranging his notices. They talked for a few minutes and then wished each other well. John only had a short walk from the church to the side gate at the west of the church before he rejoined the main street that took him back to the cottage. He tipped the large metal latch and entered his home. That was the last time he was seen alive.

—⁓—

Two

The candle was still lit in the parlour. Its dim glow cast a yellow sheen on the wet pathway at the back of the cottage. Nearby a fox cried out, which would have startled anyone else but the young boy making his way towards the cottage. On his shoulder he carried a small sack of firewood. He had been awake since four that morning and had been soaked to the skin by the relentless rain that had swept across the North Downs overnight. As he approached the wood store he couldn't but help notice that the back door into the Akehurst's cottage was ajar. Curious, once he had safely stowed away his delivery, he poked his nose into the back room. The room smelt a little damp and he could see that the embers of the fire in the hearth were only just alight and were a little smoky. He saw a cat asleep on the rocking chair and the sound of him leaning against the door alarmed it. It stood up quickly, but soon recognised him and jumped to the floor running its body against his legs.

He didn't want to make a disturbance and was about to turn back when he just then caught sight of two feet, their white soles upturned, jutting into the room. He was shocked. It was clear to him that something wasn't right, and so he turned away hastily and ran to the end of the path.

'Pa! Pa!,' he cried in a muted shout so as not to awaken the street. His father seemed not to hear him, and so he ran swiftly up to the adjoining cottage, where his father was repositioning stacks of wood in the wood store.

'Pa! Pa! Come, there's something wrong next door.'

'What is it?'

'Pa, there's something wrong next door. I think someone's fallen down or something.'

His father noted the tone of his son's voice and sensed quickly that he needed to follow. They both made their way to the back of the Akehurst's cottage, hesitated for a second at the back door, and then quietly opened the door fully and stepped inside.

'See Pa,' he said pointing.

By now the man's eyes had become accustomed to the light and he could see quite clearly two feet on the floor ahead of him, and then down the passage into the front of the house he spotted a man lying face down.

'Stay there,' he said softly to his son as he stepped gingerly across the parlour.

He was shocked when he saw Elizabeth Haine's body lying at the entrance to the front room. Her right arm was underneath her and her body lay contorted with her head held uncomfortably to one side. He could see a large dark patch on the side of her face, which he assumed was blood. She had a gazed expression.

He stepped carefully over her feet and with caution took the three small steps that brought him to John Akehurst. He was lying leaden on the stone floor. His head was to one side so that his right cheek was facing upwards. His right arm was outstretched and the other was locked heavily under his left shoulder. Although he looked peaceful the man could see that he had been hit on the back of the head. Blood had matted his grey hair, and had also streamed from his nose, which looked damaged and broken.

Turning, the man made his way to the back of the cottage, from where his son had been watching. He ushered him out and onto the street. It was only then that he realised he was starting to sweat and that he was having difficulty breathing. He paused and inhaled deeply several times.

'Son, take the cart back home as quick as you can. Go and tell your mother that I've gone to find the police and that I'll be back as soon as I can. Good boy, off you go now.'

With that he turned and ran to the end of the street, running towards the local tavern. Within two or three minutes he was at the south end of the village, where there was a police house. His knock shook the door and would have woken everyone inside. He didn't have to stand there for long before he could see the flicker of a candle as someone descended heavily footed downstairs.

The bolts were shot noisily top and bottom of the heavy door and in its frame now stood Robert Hall.

'Robert, there've been murders at the Akehurst's,' the man said, 'it looks like both of them have been attacked during the night. Come.'

Although it had seemed a long time for him to return to the cottage it was just ten minutes since he had left it. By now first light was beginning to show and the rain had stopped. The trees dripped and the leaves underfoot felt slippery and treacherous as they had both walked briskly through the village to the back entrance of the cottage. As they entered he could see anxiety on the face of the constable. The constable shone his lamp into the room and saw the two bodies which the man had described as they had approached. It was evident to him that the two had met a violent and savage death, and once he had looked more closely at first Elizabeth Haines and then John Akehurst it was clear to him also that both had been assaulted and each had received the blow of a heavy object to the back of the head. The constable felt dizzy and slightly nauseous, but had the presence when he turned to the man to not display this.

'We need to secure the cottage now,' he said a little falteringly. 'I suggest that we make sure that the front door is secure and then leave by the back locking up as best we can when we go. I'll then go straight into Leatherhead to the Union Hall to speak to the chief constable. You go home now, but please do not discuss what you have seen with anyone. I shall come and see you as soon as I can to get a statement from you.'

They then secured the cottage without further comment and took leave of each other.

*****

The constable had been in service for two years. He remembered fondly his passing out parade and the warm words his father had said to him as he stood close after the ceremony. His life in the force had been fairly routine since then, interspersed with catching petty thieves and dealing with vagrants that wandered the countryside nearby. He had not had to deal with anything like this before, and he certainly was not accustomed to seeing the trauma that he had just witnessed so vividly. He vomited in the ditch.

Within the hour he was at Union Hall. The journey had helped calm him and he prepared himself as he turned the corner into the station yard to meet his colleagues and the chief constable. As he climbed the steps to the office he heard another officer call to him across the yard. He turned and waved at him rather weakly and then pushed the door into the musty warmth. At the front desk was a young officer who looked up from his work.

'Good morning constable Hall.'

'Morning. Is the chief constable available, I need to see him as a matter of urgency please?'

'Let me enquire,' and with that he got up and made his way through the heavy wooden doors behind him. His steps echoed on the wooden boards marking his progress to the main office. He heard the rap on the chief constable's door and the muffled sound 'enter', and then after what seemed an eternity the officer's returning steps.

'He'll see you now.'

'Thank you.'

As Robert Hall entered the room he was struck at first by the clouded atmosphere in the chief constable's office. The man was a pipe smoker and had a penchant for trying new varieties of tobacco. At this time in the morning the sweet smell of the colonial weed scented the air and pervaded all it contacted. He did all he could to not wretch again.

'Sir. I have to report grave news of two murders in Bookham this morning.'

'Have you come directly from there?'

'Yes, sir. Straight from the house of John Akehurst and his housekeeper Elizabeth Haines, sir. There, sir, I discovered about an hour ago two of them, both murdered. Both had been struck on the head. They were found by a boy and his father as they were delivering firewood to the cottage at about dawn. There was no sign of forced entry to the cottage. The door at the back of the cottage had been left ajar, which is how the boy first discovered it.'

He listened calmly but as he did so he could not help but note that the constable clearly was shaken, and that his face was ashen. Even slightly green.

'Go and see the superintendent. Give him the details. Ask him to arrange a party to go up to Bookham within the hour. And then take yourself to the refectory to get something to eat. You need to be ready for what is going to be a difficult day. Well done. Call me as soon as the carriage is ready to leave.'

*****

The arrangements were made speedily for the constable to be accompanied back up to Bookham by the superintendent, a second constable and the chief constable himself. And so Robert Hall soon found himself wedged, rather uncomfortably, against the side of the carriage as it lumbered and lurched up the track towards the village. Little was said although the driver, a cheerful man most of the time, cussed constantly at one of the horses. When they got to the top of the hill and the track turned west he could see ahead of him the church spire at Bookham and to his right and in the far distance he could hear thunder. The skies had darkened by the time the party arrived in the village and turned towards John Akehurst's cottage. As the horses came to a rather shuddering halt the heavens opened again.

The village was no longer quiet. Their entry into it and their arrival at the cottage had only heightened the curiosity of the crowd that had now gathered nearby. Although he could hear their mutterings no one actually spoke to him as he led the party down the alley that ran to the back of the cottage. The path, soaking earlier that morning, was now full of puddles, which were beginning to merge and were running along the track. With his boots sodden and muddied he reopened the door and carefully stepped once again inside.

He felt calmer. Stepping forward he could see Elizabeth Haines as he had left her and ahead the pitiful sight of John Akehurst. His features now seemed very haggard and his deathly expression seemed more shocked and frightened than he had appeared on first view. The blood around his head and on the tiled floor had become a dirtier and darker red and was now dry. The superintendent had followed him into the cottage and stood stiffly at Robert Hall's side. The constable could feel his tension. He remained silent, for the moment, as he viewed the scene. He scanned the room, which was darkened by the gloom outside and noted that there had been a fire in the hearth, but that this was now barely aglow. The two bodies were lying as the constable had described. The first, a woman who looked small and thin and possibly aged about sixty lay ahead of him. She had on a white bonnet, soiled ruby with her own blood, and a nightdress. Next to her right arm lay a woollen shawl. Her head had been battered behind her right ear.

He stepped forward towards the second body, which he knew was John Akehurst. He recognised the man whom he had seen only two weeks earlier seated at the front of the church in Bookham. He looked crumpled as he lay there, his arm twisted under his strong frame. He had been beaten and his face evidently had been hit hard as the constable had described. His cheeks still retained the ruddy colour that the superintendent had remarked to himself when he had seen John Akehurst alive, but his skin now had a darker hue, more purple than red.

The superintendent turned and looked at the chief constable, who had now also entered the cottage, and whose frame blocked the doorway. He acknowledged him and then instructed the constable who had come with them to keep watch outside. He turned to Robert Hall. The look they gave one another then was expressive and indicated both shock and keen awareness that they were at the start of a difficult journey together.

'Fine,' said the superintendent. 'Constable, prepare a written description of each victim and the surrounds. Identify and secure any items, which might have been used or might provide us with insight or evidence. Then have the victims removed from here and taken to Union Hall for examination by the police doctor. I shall have a wagon sent up here as soon as I am back at Union Hall. Clear?'

'Sir,' Robert Hall answered.

Then as swiftly as they had entered the superintendent and chief constable departed. Robert Hall heard their carriage move away from the front of the cottage and he was left alone to survey the morbid remains.

—⟋⟍—

THREE

Mary Ayres awoke. Hers had been a fitful sleep, with the rain relentless all night long. It had soaked the ground around the tent in which she and Will lay. She had meant to mend the tear that had appeared in its upper end about two weeks ago, but the weather had been fine for so long that she hadn't yet got round to it. 'What a shame,' she thought to herself with a wry smile, partly mocking her own laziness, and a little amused at the unnecessary inconvenience that it now caused her.

She could hear running water. It seemed faster than it had been when they had pitched the tent there the previous day. The river below Box Hill she had always thought was beautiful and she had enjoyed playing down there as a small child. Now grown up she still had the same emotions about the place. Their tent was close to the stepping stones across the river, which allowed them access to the paths opposite where they were able to walk when they had time. But now Mary had to rush. Today she needed to walk into Dorking, where she had arranged with the local church to have a stand at the church fete. She had her paintings ready, but had done little preparation for the event. She felt a tiny bit anxious.

Time seemed to have slipped by so quickly since yesterday when they had returned to the area. Once they had arranged the tent they had walked up the hill through West Humble and down into Bookham. As they walked along the main street towards the church Mary was amazed at how many old friends she had met. They all seemed very pleased to see her and her girlfriends appeared impressed with Will, who stood for the most part quietly at her side. When they got to the church they had turned left towards her mother's dwelling. As they turned the corner she could see the gate to her grandfather's cottage a little way down the adjacent road and she reminded herself that she was going to see him the next day after she had finished in Dorking.

Her mother's house was down a short dirt track off the main road. The garden was overgrown with bind weed covering most of the large shrubs that filled the front. The gate was off one of its hinges and leant rather sadly to one side. As she walked down the path Mary could see the dim light of a candle through the window. Her mother always kept the door slightly open to let her cats out and so Mary walked straight into the dwelling unannounced.

'Mother, I'm home,' she shouted.

At first there wasn't a reply, but then her mother appeared from the back. She was still carrying the wet clothes that she had been hanging outside and she looked agitated at first. But on seeing Mary her demeanour changed in an instant.

'Mary, Mary, Mary,' she repeated as she gave her daughter a kiss on her right cheek. 'Where have you been for the past few weeks then? Hello Will.'

From that moment her chatter didn't stop until they left about five hours later.

*****

By the time Mary and Will left it was beginning to get fairly dark. The sky was heavy with grey clouds and it looked like rain was on its way. They walked briskly up the street towards the church, passed the tavern and towards a farm at the top of the hill above Leatherhead. From there they were able to follow a track through woods, which straddled the escarpment, before descending down the steep slope towards the bridge close to Mickleham. They stopped at the tavern there for a rest and to get something to eat. To Mary's surprise the barmaid was an old school friend. Although they hadn't been particularly close at school they chatted while the food was prepared and the girl then unwittingly remarked on how untidy Mary looked.

'You're right,' Mary said dismissively.

'How did you get blood and a tear on that sleeve,' she then went on to say.

'Oh, that was me slipping on the way down here against a fence. It really hurt.'

She didn't make any other comments about it, but was also aware that Will, who had been introduced to her earlier, had had little to say for himself and seemed the whole time engrossed in his own thoughts. He too looked just as dishevelled, and she noticed that the knuckles of his hands seemed sore and dirty. Having eaten they said their goodbyes and set off just as the rain started to fall. Running most of the way they soon reached their tent. Already some of their blankets and covers were damp, but they made light of it and soon settled down beside each other. Lying close to get warm she could feel Will's body against hers and heard his steady breathing as she drifted off to sleep.

*****

John Akehurst's body was the first to be brought out of the cottage. It was carried with immense care by four young police constables through the front door and onto the adjoining road where the police carriage was stood. The two horses, a grey and a chestnut, were edgy. Their temperament was being tested by the crowd that by now was milling around the area, creating an additional tension that had not been present a few hours earlier. Once his body had been laid on the left of the carriage, the constables made their way back up the path and into the cottage. A short time later they appeared again, this time with the slighter body of Elizabeth Haines, who was now shrouded in a large colourful wrap that she had made for herself the previous year. Gently the officers placed her alongside John Akehurst. The transfer completed, the carriage driver shut and bolted the carriage's back door and returned to his seat at the front, where he waited for his instruction to return to Union Hall.

The sight of Elizabeth Haines' body and the solemn manner, in which the constables had completed their task and then, as a single disciplined unit, had taken their positions alongside the carriage, had quietened the watching crowd. Two young children squealed as they played on the grass opposite the cottage, but hastily were admonished and subdued by one of the adults close to them. At that point the officer in charge called the carriage party, which had been stood rigidly to attention at the back of the carriage, to order. He then gave the instruction to move. The driver unlocked the brake and spoke a softened command to the horses. The carriage lurched as the horses took the strain and then it started its steady progress up the lane towards the church and the crossroads at the centre of the village. Most of those viewing now stood very still, but several others ran on ahead, noisily, keen to see as much of the event as they could. As the carriage approached the corner and made to turn left, the church bell began to peel a dull, solemn call. That drew visible emotion from the onlookers who were stood in some numbers outside the tavern, and there were cries of 'God Bless you both' from several bystanders. The carriage steadily made its way down the road towards Leatherhead, and in a short time was nearly out of sight. The driver could still hear behind him the bell, which rang for a further five minutes until Father Bolland began to feel faint from the exertion, at which point it stopped.

The tavern was busy. There was little talked about other than how John Akehurst and his housekeeper had been killed in this of all villages. Speculation soon began to float around the public house as to who might have committed such a terrible act. There were those who thought that perhaps John Akehurst had been killed by someone whom he had helped convict in the past, and who recently had left prison intent on doing him harm. Others voiced the opinion that it was probably a casual robbery gone wrong, for it had often been mooted that he kept some of his alleged 'fortune' in cash in the cottage.

In the cottage meantime Robert Hall calmly completed his report. He sat in the large wooden chair close to the front window, from where he had witnessed the bodies being placed in the carriage. During his time there he had heard the crowd gather outside. Intent on his duties he had not allowed himself to be distracted by it. But now he relaxed a little and watched as the spectators thinned and made their way back into the village. When he had finally finished writing his report, in which he described the scene in the cottage and the condition in which he had found the two occupants earlier that morning, he called in the constable, who was still stood patiently alone at the back of the cottage. He entered looking rather cold and drawn.

'Right. I'm finished here for the time being. I shall make my way to Union Hall to post my report. You should stay here until someone comes to relieve you later this afternoon. Secure the back door and keep the front door locked.'

'Sir.'

Rising from the seat, Robert Hall collected his papers and then walked carefully to the front door, before turning to take a final look at the scene. The cottage was now lightened by the sun, which shone weakly through the back window. He was struck how everything appeared normal. Coats hung on pegs. Boots cleaned and carefully stowed on racks. Ornaments around the fire, which now was dull and grey. As he stood there he felt a nudge against his left leg. Looking down he saw Elizabeth Haines' cat nuzzling him. He bent down and ran his fingers along its back. The cat purred loudly, and then jumped onto the warm seat he had just left, where it settled.

'Until later then,' he said to the constable as he opened the front door.

'Sir.'

Walking up the lane he could see ahead of him Father Bolland. They greeted each other in a subdued way each conscious of the circumstances in which they met. Robert Hall informed the priest that he had completed a report of the scene for the chief constable, whom he was on his way to see and the priest advised that he would be holding a vigil in the church that afternoon for John Akehurst and Elizabeth Haines. Robert Hall then walked up through the village back to his house. In the kitchen was his wife. She appeared sad and thoughtful and looked at him as if she herself had been hurt, and so he gave her a hug. She burst into tears. Once she had calmed herself he explained that he had to go to Union Hall and would be back as soon as he could.

'Who knows,' he had said to her questioning as to who might have killed the two of them. 'And no, I do not understand what the motive might have been.' Normally his wife would not have interrogated him as anxiously, but she was so upset by the event that had happened in their lovely village that she could not on this occasion restrain her intense curiosity.

Robert Hall grabbed an apple and went to the back of the house, where his horse was stabled. He got her ready and then set off for Leatherhead. Taking the road north of the village he headed down the escarpment to the river. Crossing it he could see that it had swollen overnight and was now running fast. He stopped for a minute or two, ate his apple, throwing the core into the swell, before moving on towards Union Hall. There he sensed the increased level of activity since his visit earlier that day. The police carriage stood outside, its gate down, the contents now elsewhere, and the horses unhitched and taken to the stables. He saw the police doctor's trap parked at the side of the building. He knew the doctor would most probably have started his examination of the bodies by this time. Having hitched his horse he again made his way up the stairs into the building and as he approached the front desk the constable seated there recognised and acknowledged him. He told him that the chief constable was expecting him, and that he should go through straightaway to make his report. As he walked down the corridor he again could smell that same distinctive odour. Knocking on the door he heard the chief constable shout 'Enter.'

The market in Dorking had been busy as usual that morning, although one might have thought that the inclement weather earlier in the day would have deterred most. Trade at all of the stalls had been brisker than usual.

Mary too had enjoyed the day, but by early afternoon she felt that she probably had had most of that day's business. She could see that many shoppers were now making for the taverns in the main street, which ran close by the church, or were setting off for home. She collected her belongings and put the small bundle over her right shoulder.

'See you next time,' she shouted to the stallholder across the way from her. He replied with a cheery wave.

She set off retracing the steps that she had taken earlier that day heading down to the river. The ground on which she and Will had pitched their tent yesterday was now bare, Will having packed it up and set off to walk to Oxshott that morning. He and Mary planned to meet there the following day. In the late autumn sun the walk beside the river was invigorating, but Mary soon began to tire. Fortunately her luck was in, for as she reached Mickleham once again a builder's wagon approached and the driver offered her a lift part of the way. She got off at Leatherhead, and as she passed Union Hall she was surprised to see how busy it was there. She thought little more of it until she neared the top of the hill approaching Bookham, where she met Mrs Marshall, whom she had known since she was a small child. Mrs Marshall was surprised but pleased to see her, although Mary thought she seemed on edge.

Once they had greeted each other she said, 'I'm so sorry about your grandfather and Miss Haines.'

Mary didn't understand what she meant and Mrs Marshall immediately comprehended that too when she saw Mary's reaction.

'Oh! You haven't heard then?' she continued having quickly gathered her thoughts.

'Heard what?'

'I am so sorry Mary. A terrible thing has happened in the village. During the night your grandfather and his friend died. It seems there was a break in at the cottage and they were both attacked. The police have been at the house since first light. Just a few hours ago they took them both away to Union Hall.'

Mary stood silent. Shocked, disbelieving, staring at her friend. She drew breath and now could feel her heart pounding, and her chest tightening.

'That explains why it seemed so busy when I passed by there just now. Where's my mother?'

'I don't know dear. I haven't seen her today. Why don't you go to the village and find her?' Then sympathetically she added, ' I'm sure she will be dreadfully upset.'

Mary couldn't remember what they had said to each other after that, but very soon she was on her way again, walking as fast as her legs would take her. As she came passed the church she heard someone call her name, and turning towards the voice she could see down the path leading to the church Father Bolland, with her mother. Her mother ran towards her and threw her arms around Mary's neck. She was inconsolable. Father Bolland joined them and he too put his arms around them both and spoke softly to them trying to bring them some comfort.

They walked together towards the church and on entering Mary and her mother lit a candle each, placing it at the feet of the statue of the Virgin Mary, which stood at the entrance. They walked with the priest towards the altar and he settled them in their usual pew. He knelt beside them both and started to say the Lord's Prayer. They eventually joined with him, speaking it softly to themselves. They stayed kneeling for several minutes in silence until their thoughts were interrupted by footsteps entering the church as two elderly ladies, chatting, came inside to attend to the flowers. They then both sat without speaking a little while longer before moving out of the pew, crossing themselves, making their way towards the back of the church. Mary and her mother thanked the priest for his kindness. He then told them he was having a vigil at dusk and that he would pray for them both, for the souls of the two departed, and their families.

Mary took her mother's hand and they walked slowly back up the path and down the main road towards her mother's dwelling. When they got there the light was beginning to fade and their minds were soon preoccupied with getting a fire going in the hearth and with fetching fresh water from the nearby well. They didn't speak to each other much again during that evening. Each was clearly distressed, happy to have company, but content to have time to think.

—⁓—

Four

A solitary light was all that Charles Card had in his office. The fire in the hearth burned gently and gave him some warmth as he sat in his large high back leather chair to one side of it. He raised his crystal goblet and sipped the whisky he had poured a few minutes earlier. His third that evening. He found it helped him to relax and to think. He could hear sounds some distance away in the building and occasionally down the corridor outside his office door. But the frantic activity, which had punctuated the day, had now subsided. He looked at the clock, which hung on the wall opposite. It was eleven thirty.

His mind settled a little as he sat there, quietly, watching the embers flicker and shift. He lent forward, picked up a small log from the basket and placed it carefully onto the fire. It crackled as its sap started to burn. He wiped his hand on the side of his trousers, before downing what was left in his glass. He got up and made his way across the room, where he poured himself another drink.

He started to pace and as he did so the wooden boards echoed his tread and his leather boots creaked softly at his every step. His mind began to race again as he reviewed where his officers had got to today investigating the murders at Bookham. He went through the events as they had progressed during the day and he reflected on the instructions that he had given his superintendent that morning. He wasn't entirely pleased. The male victim was a well known figure in the local community and his housekeeper too was highly regarded for her kindnesses. There was an expectation that their aggressors would be caught quickly and that justice would be done. But the first day had brought little in the way of leads for his officers to follow. The crime scene had not revealed anything that was of value, although he did retain at the front of his mind the advice that he had been given by the police doctor about three hours earlier that both victims had died from a head wound delivered by what he thought was a metal object, which had two sharp raised points. The result was that each victim had had their skull punctured in two places about an inch apart.

The chief constable had ordered all roads within the district be watched to a radius of ten miles, and that anyone travelling along them be stopped and questioned. He had been informed earlier that evening that one hundred and twenty five people had been stopped but nothing of value had so far come from this activity. Most of those questioned travelled frequently going about their business, and were known to his officers. At least a quarter, however, were described in the report he had read as vagrants, with no known residence in the area. A search of their belongings had not revealed anything noteworthy or suspicious to the investigating officers.

He placed the glass on his desk, collected his keys, opened his door and stepped into the corridor. Looking to his right he could see an officer sat at the front desk, apparently busy with paperwork. He turned and walked in the other direction, taking the steps, which led him down towards the cells. At the bottom of the steps he found himself stood outside a door marked Police Doctor. He knew the room was locked the doctor having gone home several hours earlier. Unlocking the door he reached inside for the oil lamp, which was placed on the table at the entrance. He struck a match, which eerily lit the room and then lit the wick. He could see on the heavy wooden table opposite the body of John Akehurst and Elizabeth Haines. Each had been shrouded carefully with a large linen sheet. These had settled and now revealed clearly the outline of their torsos. He couldn't help but remark to himself how heavy John Akehurst had become; and as if by sharp contrast how frail and fragile his image of Elizabeth seemed. He settled himself close to them and gently raised the linen sheet covering John Akehurst's head. He could see the bruising behind his ear and by crouching and looking upwards with the oil lamp held close he saw quite clearly the distinct marking and puncture points. He stared for a minute or so, but wasn't able to determine from what he had seen how such holes might have been made. He replaced the linen, straightening it, before moving around the table to where Elizabeth Haines lay. Once again he lifted the linen, and was taken aback by the trauma that he could see still reflected in her face. He knelt on his right knee, and held the oil lamp just above his head. The light flickered warmly on her pale face. He stared at her for a few seconds, before dropping his gaze to the area just below her ear, where once again he saw similar puncture wounds. He raised himself up, adjusted the linen which settled softly on her face, and then stepped back half a pace, standing tall. Not an outwardly emotional man, he felt himself holding in some of the feelings he was having. Breathing deeply he whispered 'God bless you both. And may your souls rest in peace, forever,' and then stood motionless for a time before gathering himself, and turning towards the door. He switched off the oil lamp, watched it go out, and then stepped outside. Having locked the door, he turned the handle to make sure the room was secure, and then retraced his steps back to his office.

Sat at his desk he made a note of his visit to the police doctor's room and what he had witnessed there. Then having drunk the remnants of the whisky that he had left on the desk earlier, he stood up, moved to a couch he had at the far end of his office, where he lay down. Very soon he was fast asleep.

It was a feeling of cramp in his right leg that awoke him. He glanced at the clock and saw that it was now just past five. It was still dark outside although light from the courtyard opposite his office illuminated it casting shadows across his floor and on the wall next to him. He lay there for five or ten minutes gathering his strength, before rising and leaving the room. On his way out of the building he acknowledged the desk officer and said that he would be back in a couple of hours, knowing that he had arranged a meeting to review progress on the investigation for eight that morning. The street was silent and the pavements were still wet from the rain that had continued to fall overnight. A large fox ran across the road ahead of him and buried itself quickly into the undergrowth.

His house was just a short walk from Union Hall in a well to do area of Leatherhead. He had lived there with his wife and two young daughters since arriving in the town to take up his posting some four years earlier. They had settled in well he thought as he approached the house, although it was not exactly convenient for his wife, whose family was in Suffolk. While it did not bother him unduly, she found their absence hard to bear at times.

He climbed the five steps at the front of the house with care, treading gingerly so as not to make too much noise, and he did the same as he unlocked the front door and entered the hallway. Although the house was warmer than the air outside he could feel that it was chilled. He took off his boots and placed them on a rack in the hall before moving to the back where the larder and kitchen was situated. His dog stirred in its basket and then sighed. He bent down and patted its head gently before moving to the larder where he found a pitcher of milk. He poured himself a glass and downed it. Its iciness shocked his system.

On his way upstairs the dog, by now alert, ran up against his leg and reached the top before him and stood there, tail wagging furiously. He patted him again as he passed it and entered the bedroom at the back of the house, where he could see his wife asleep under heavy covers. She stirred as he undressed, placing his uniform on a frame that he had positioned near the window. He slipped into the bed and felt instantly the warmth contained there. His wife turned and whispered a soft hello to him. The dog settled by his feet.

The sound of two girls playing woke him about two hours later. He got up without hesitation realising that he had little time before he needed to be back in his office. As his wife lay asleep he washed, shaved and dressed. He looked in on the two girls, putting a finger to his mouth as he entered so that they would keep quiet.

'Hello you two. Don't wake your mother. I shall see you later.'

They smiled at him and then carried on playing with their toys.

Leaving the house he decided to take a different route back, which allowed him to walk alongside the river. After a few minutes he regretted having made that choice as his boots were soon muddied. He swore under his breath.

*****

Union Hall was now busy again. A police wagon was in the yard and he could see three men being taken from it to the basement door, which led to the holding cell. His superintendent was at the front desk looking tired, clearly not having slept much that night. He looked pleased.

'Good morning, sir. I've just returned from the Oxshott area, where we apprehended three men. I've brought them in for questioning as they didn't seem to be able to explain their movements during yesterday.'

'Very good. I'll see you at eight for a full report then.'

'Sir.'

Meanwhile the three men, looking dishevelled and smelling not too fresh, were taken to the cell below them. This had no window, was stonewalled, which by now were damp from the heavy rains that had fallen during the past thirty six hours. The floor was muddy and had sodden straw strewn around it. In one corner of the room a solitary man sat crumpled, his hands manacled. He was chained to the wall. He barely acknowledged their arrival.

The three were bundled in without much ceremony. Standing there together in the centre they watched as the rusted metal gate was shut and locked. After several minutes their eyes had become more accustomed to the room and they could see a running tap on one wall and close to it a hole, blackened with faeces. The stench shocked their senses when they first arrived, and still did even after they had been there awhile. There wasn't much else to do other than settle themselves and wait to see what fate would bring them.

Above them, the chief constable was rereading the reports of his investigating officers again in preparation for his meeting. At eight his superintendent and three officers knocked and entered, and then stood in front of his desk.

'At ease, gentlemen,' he said without looking up.

When he had finished reading the page he raised his eyes, looked at them intently, and then asked for an update. There was little to please him. The roads had been blocked and anyone travelling had been questioned. Nothing of consequence had been discovered as yet, although the three men who had been apprehended did seem to show some anxiety when they had been approached on a trail east of Oxshott late last night.

'Well you had better find out what they have to say,' he barked. 'Get to it.'

Once they had left the office the superintendent instructed two of his officers to start questioning the three men and to report back by early afternoon. In the meantime he said he and the other officer would return to Bookham to continue questioning villagers there.

At his desk the chief constable still sat morosely. He bit his lip until it bled, and then kicked the side of his desk, chipping it. This was not going to be another happy day he said aloud to himself.

The three men were rather surprised that the officers had returned so quickly. They stood up, falteringly, as the gate was unlocked. The officers approached one of the men and each grabbing an arm heaved him out of the cell roughly, banging his head against the heavy bars as they took him away down the corridor and into an adjoining room. The two that were left settled themselves again, but soon they were looking at each other uneasily on hearing the other's cries of pain and the officers shouting abuse at him.

Ten minutes later he was dragged down the corridor and thrown onto the floor, where he lay motionless, heaving for breath. They didn't move until the men had locked the gate and their footsteps indicated that they had reached the top of the stairs.

'Alright, easy, easy,' said one of the men as he helped his friend to sit up. He held his head up and placed an arm around his shoulders.

'Ah !,' the other cried, feeling the bruises. 'Seems there's been a murder at Bookham,' he said. 'Two old dears attacked the other night they said. They think we might know something about it.'

As he listened Will was shocked by the news, but there wasn't much he could do now, he thought, other than let events look after themselves here.

When the officers returned they were less brutal this time. They opened the cell door and beckoned Will to step out. They took him to the same room that the first man had been in, but if he had been expecting a beating he was to be pleasantly surprised. The officers calmly asked him who he was, where he was going to and where he had come from in the previous two days. He gave the same answers as he had done earlier to them when they had stopped him at the roadside. He could see that they had brought with them his tool bag. They asked him to show them what he carried in it, and he did so, taking care and trying to remain polite and assured in his speech. As he took out each tool he explained its purpose. They showed some interest in a tool that was larger than the others, which he explained he would use for stretching leather, but after handling it for a little while they simply gave it back to him.

The senior officer then said, ' You can go now.'

And with that instruction the other officer escorted him down the corridor and up the stairs and out into the yard.

He gave Will a shove and said,

'On your way, boy.'

*****

Will didn't know what might happen to the other two men brought to Union Hall with him that day, and he didn't want to stay around to find out. The walk up the hill from the town towards Bookham seemed steeper than usual. Perhaps it was because he was tired not having slept since the previous night and having been cold and frightened all night. By the time he reached the top he was sweating and drawing heavily for breath. He stopped and turned to view where he had come from and could see ahead of him in the distance a thin line of smoke from a cottage by the river, which was curling up slowly in a gentle spiral in the cold air. He smiled to himself, pleased that he was free again and looking forward to surprising Mary. He walked the short distance into the village and was taken aback by the number of people out and about at that time of the morning. The tavern was already open for business and seemed to be fairly full. He thought he would stop for a quick drink to warm himself and have a bite to eat as he hadn't eaten anything since he finished off a pie in the police wagon about ten hours earlier. It was certainly busy. Many of the people there he recognised but there were many others that he didn't, and whom he thought seemed out of place.

'Hello Edith,' he said to the landlady, who was clearing tables as he approached the bar, 'you're very busy this morning'

'Hello Will. How are you?' And then she told him that since the murders yesterday the place had been inundated with police investigators asking questions and had been swamped by reporters from around the county. 'There's even a reporter from The Times, see over there, him with the smart topcoat and hat. Imagine that?' And with that off she went, briskly, to the kitchen before he could to speak to her further.

At the bar Will ordered himself a local ale and a meat pie and then stood looking at the strangers seated at the nearby tables. He was deep in thought when a familiar voice interrupted him.

'Well if it isn't my old friend Will. How are you old boy?'

Will turned and there was an old friend Guy Soden, whom he had known since he was a child. Guy seemed much stockier than he remembered him and his hair was thinner and greying at the temples. They soon fell into their old familiar conversation, interrupted for a short time only by the consumption without much style of a large fairly stale and overcooked pie. When Will realised that he had better get on his way to see Mary before she left to meet him in Oxshott as they had planned, he started to take his leave and in doing so mentioned her name. Guy was taken aback at this piece of news, but tried not to show surprise. Of course he was aware of what had happened in the village, and vaguely knew the family Will was speaking about, but he certainly hadn't appreciated until then that Will was close to the relative of one of the victims. He couldn't believe his luck as he thought what his editor might say of his contacts here.

'Stay a little while longer; another drink?' he said seeking to inveigle Will to delay his departure.

'No I mustn't,' Will said, still unaware of his friend's particular interest or indeed his current profession.

'Mary Ayres?' he said casually, 'is that the girl who went to school with us, and who had a relative who was a lawyer sometime down in the town? John...'

'Akehurst,' Will interrupted.

'Yes.'

'Oh,' he hesitated for a second or two, then as sympathetically as he could said, 'sorry Will, but I've got some bad news for you. It's John Akehurst everyone here's talking about at present; he was murdered with his housekeeper two nights ago.'

Will's earlier shock now turned to real concern. Concern for Mary of course; but also her mother.

'Look I must go,' he said abruptly.

'Well later; perhaps this evening?' Guy retorted insensitively.

'Maybe. Look I must go. See you around.' And with that Will collected his belongings and was gone.

It didn't take him long to get to Mary's mother's dwelling. The atmosphere there was as bad as he had anticipated. He found Mary by the stove in the back room, stirring a bowl of oatmeal slowly so as not to burn or overcook it. She was taken aback at first as he came through the door, but was pleased to see him. She hadn't forgotten that she was expecting to see him in Oxshott later that day, but hadn't the energy to think about how she was going to let him know that things had changed in the last twenty four hours, and that she wouldn't be able to be there. She told him that; and he told her that he was so sorry about her grandfather, and then he explained how he had been taken in by the police in Oxshott and brought to Union Hall overnight for questioning, before being sent on his way a little while ago.

'What would they want to question you about? ' she said indignantly.

'Nothing. I was just stopped at a road block about a mile from Oxshott. There were two other men there at the time, looking a little worse for wear, perhaps a little suspicious too, and I got hauled in with them.'

'What happened?'

'They just took us to Union Hall, threw us into a cell; you should have seen the place; and then having asked me a few questions and looked at my belongings let me go.'

'Well at least you're here now,' she said, leaning against him and kissing him gently and affectionately on his right cheek. 'Mother's upstairs asleep. She's distraught. She's never going to get over this I'm sure.'

They talked for a little while longer while Mary ate her oatmeal, until they could hear Mary's mother moving around above them.

'Mother. Are you up? Will's here.'

The only reply they heard was the sound of sobbing.

*****

Mary's mother wasn't really a sentimental person. She possibly had reason to be, but she had conditioned herself to be strong and forward looking, practical and pragmatic. Traits she had most likely also inherited from her father. As an only child her father had taken great care to ensure that she understood the world around her and to comprehend that unlike some of the stories that he read her during her early years, life had a way of not delivering the honeyed endings described there. He had hoped that she might follow him into his law practice, and so in her teens he had taken to telling her about some of the cases that he was handling, and had even had her accompany him into court, where she had sat passively to one side listening to the arguments presented and hearing for herself the disappointing details of other peoples' lives.

Her life hadn't however followed the path that John Akehurst had hoped for her. Always independent and strong willed Eleanor Ayres (n. Akehurst) hadn't really settled to the studies that were required to achieve his ambitions. Instead she had spent most of her time thinking about and enjoying being an active part of the local community, where she was involved with a choir and a drama club. Although not an accomplished actress, she nevertheless had had some success with several minor roles and had really enjoyed those. But her real interest lay in designing and preparing the costumes. It was here that she learnt her seamstress skills for which she was now noted.

It was also in the theatre that she met Philip Ayres. Taking the lead in many of the productions he was a handsome and accomplished amateur actor, with something of a reputation for romancing his cast members. It did not come as a surprise to anyone really when he and Eleanor struck up a strong relationship. What did shock was her pregnancy, which she was very soon unable to hide within the company, or indeed from her father. Disappointed at first by this turn of events John Akehurst was later pleasantly surprised that Philip stuck by Eleanor and with his blessing had married her in the early summer of 1806.

The young couple enjoyed life together but were not well off. And so John Akehurst helped them out, setting them both up in a dwelling he had acquired, and in which she now still lived. Eleanor undertook seamstress work within the community and fortunately also enjoyed the patronage of John Mullay, who had a large estate in nearby Polesden, which kept her busy. Philip meantime had secured employment with the stagecoach business, which ran a regular service between London and the Royal dockyards in Portsmouth. A staging post on the route had been recently established at Ripley, where there was a large stable and a good hostelry for the travellers. His task was to look after the horses ensuring that replacement teams were ready to take over from those travelling in either direction.

Life for them had a comfortable, predictable routine for the next five years, during which time they enjoyed seeing Mary grow into a charming little girl. Then late one evening in 1812 Philip tragically was trapped against a stable wall by a horse he was harnessing. With his hip and left leg broken he suffered severe shock. Days later additional complications in his condition killed him. He was just twenty nine years old. Since that time Eleanor had again relied on her father for financial and moral support and had always been grateful for that. Bringing up Mary alone had not been easy for her. Over the years she had had several suitors, but each had sadly in the end been discouraged to take her to the altar by the responsibilities with which she presented them. So now in her early forties she was a widow, with little to show in the way of domestic comforts. But throughout this difficult time in her life she had still retained the indomitable spirit that her father had often commented on, and which he so admired in her. That spirit was now being once again sorely tested.

She sobbed into her pillow, but finally taking hold of her emotions she raised herself up, straightening her clothing that had become twisted and ruffled, before rising.

'Mary, darling,' she croaked, her throat sore from the past few hours, 'I'll be down in a minute or so. Then I'll make you and Will something to eat for lunch.'

'Alright mother.'

In the room below Mary and Will sat coiled, fingers caressing fingers, knees interlocked, enjoying being together once again.

When eventually she gingerly came down the wooden ladder that gave her access to the floor above she looked wrecked. Her eyes were reddened and puffy, her complexion ashen, and her general appearance out of character.

'Hello Will,' she sighed.

Will didn't say anything at first, but simply looked at her as sympathetically as he was able to muster, gave her a boyish smile, and then said,

'Everything will be alright, you'll see.'

She retorted in a scolding tone, 'What do you mean it will be alright? Nothing's going to be the same again. For us. For the village. Who were those animals that killed my father and Elizabeth? They need gutting.'

They both sat silently not wanting to inflame the atmosphere further. Then after what seemed minutes, but was no time at all in reality, Eleanor checked herself and apologised to them both for her ill mannered outburst.

'That's alright Mrs Ayres,' Will said spontaneously. 'It's quite understandable. It's an upsetting time for you; for all of us.'

Mary stood up and gave her mother a gentle hug, before moving towards the back of the dwelling. She opened the door there, stepped outside and stood passively for several minutes.

'Why don't I make us all something to eat?'

And with that her mother busied herself, stoking the fire, which was soon burning fiercely in the hearth.

The dwelling comprised only one room on the ground floor. At the front was a small area where a heavy wooden chair, more a bench, provided seating for two. Alongside the fire Eleanor had placed a rocking chair, where she sat most of the time. A variety of pots hung in the hearth, while at the back she had a table and three chairs. The table was covered with a heavy linen drape that she had recovered from the local estate when they were completing a refurbishment there several years earlier. Some of its edges had been carefully unthreaded by a cat that had visited her over the years, but whose whereabouts she was now not sure as she hadn't seen him for a while. There was always a rather musty smell in the place, unless the fire was burning, when it then became a little smoky. She slept in the room above in a single bed placed up against the wall. Everything up there was neat and ordered. Unfortunately the absence of a window meant the room was darkened most of the time. While that made it a cosy place to be in the winter, during the summer she often had to resort to sleeping downstairs to keep herself cool.

They ate what she made in silence. When they had finished Mary suggested that she and Will should take a walk into the village, and so that's how they spent the rest of the afternoon.

The village was fairly quiet that day. People were going about their business as usual, children played their games as loudly as ever in the school playground, but there was an atmosphere of concern and upset that had not been experienced before. Having the police working their way up the main street taking statements from individuals and visiting homes in the area immediately surrounding John Akehurst's cottage was unsettling for everyone. Robert Hall had been assigned to lead the local investigating team. His knowledge of the area and of its inhabitants was seen as an asset. But it didn't seem to be helping him just yet. Although the two officers assigned to him had been very diligent and active, speaking to over one hundred and fifty people since yesterday morning, they had not yet uncovered any lead worth following. Their time today was being devoted to taking formal statements from neighbours. Their line of questioning was intended to ensure that specific details of the twelve hours prior to the murders were accounted for by each individual. It was hoped that their observations and comments would identify a possible suspect or some activity that had aroused their suspicion. But that wasn't to be. And so as he sat in the small room at the police house, which he used for his administration, he was starting to feel dismay. He turned the page on yet another statement and read the transcript, carefully written by one of his officers. Like all the others he had read that day this one too described how the individual 'had had a typical day, and while one or two strangers had been seen in the village, that was not unusual.' Anyway the statement read 'they didn't appear to be the type that would go on to murder our neighbours.'

Robert Hall knew that he had to report on his investigation to the chief constable the next morning. His meeting was scheduled for eight thirty. Although he had been shocked by the events, he could see that this presented him with an opportunity to shine and to show his professional capabilities. At first a little disquieted by his ambition surfacing so overtly, he soon overcame his concerns and focused his energies on the tasks, which needed to be completed. He rationalised his feelings by saying to himself that he was doing it for John Akehurst anyway, and John would have been proud of him. That's how he had thought at the start, but those thoughts were gradually being replaced by concern that he was not going to demonstrate any progress to the chief constable, and his steady realisation now that his career aspirations weren't so easily going to be satisfied. He leant back, relaxing into the back of his chair. He took a deep breath, raised his eyes from the desk and began to stare out of the window. He allowed his thoughts to wander aimlessly for a few seconds before gathering himself again and settling to write his report.

By four that afternoon it was beginning to get dark. His wife busied herself in their living room lighting the two lanterns they had there, and then came into his room to light the one on his desk. She knew when he was concerned about something and she noted his agitation now.

'How's it going dear,' she asked cautiously not expecting to receive too detailed a reply. Robert stopped writing and looked up, smiling at her wistfully.

'This is going to be a difficult one to sort out,' he replied, pausing for a second before going on to tell her about the various witness statements that he had read in the last half hour. 'As I said,' he continued, as she turned to leave, gently shutting the door behind her.

*****

The investigation was not proceeding any better at Union Hall. The superintendent had briefed his men earlier and the four officers assigned to him today had spent a cold and cheerless morning riding all the lanes in a radius of five miles around Bookham. They had stopped everyone travelling along the lanes to ascertain who they were, where they were coming from and going to, and asking if they had seen anything or anyone in the past two days in this area that had been suspicious. Having been outside for at least eight hours now, they each were starting to feel strained and disgruntled. They too had been made very aware by the superintendent that morning that he had high expectations of them, and was looking forward to receiving their reports that evening. As planned they met up with each other again at five at the crossroads east of Leatherhead and began to head back towards Union Hall exchanging their news as they travelled.

'He's not going to like it.'

'True. But what can we do about it? There's absolutely nothing happened around here that anyone thinks important in relation to the murders. We've all seen the travellers around here, and while anyone might have done it, there's nothing we've found to link anyone to it. We can't keep dragging in everyone who might look a bit dodgy like the others did this morning. Where's that going to get anyone?'

The other three nodded their agreement as they made their way up the road by the river. They stopped for five minutes there to let the horses drink from a trough, while they shared the last of the food, which they had taken with them when they set out that morning. One of the horses began to urinate and another let off a fart, whose smell contaminated the air for several minutes.

'That smell just about describes how I'm feeling right now,' one of them said. They all laughed loudly.

'We'd better be getting back. Soon be six.'

Heading up the road again, they began to sing a melancholy song that they had heard sung at a local tavern weeks ago, which they had all liked, and which had now become their anthem.

*****

It began to rain heavily by seven that evening and didn't relent until after midnight. Father Bolland stepped over the puddles now settled on the path to the church. He raised his cassock to stop the hem getting too muddied as he went. The church had already been lit by one of the parishioners, who helped him with his work, and so when he entered it the atmosphere the candles created was pleasing. He liked this time of day. It had for him a certain spiritual quality about it that made it rather special. He paused at the base of the statue of the Virgin Mary, crossed himself, touched her feet and put his fingers to his lips. He then made his way through the centre of the church just pausing short of the altar to cross himself again. He turned left and as he walked searched for the key to his room that he had secreted in his pocket. He unlocked the door and took hold of the lantern that had been left for him, lit, outside it. On a shelf close to his desk he had his book of sermons and books of prayers. He reached for them as he settled at his desk and began to flick through one of them, marking interesting passages with bits of torn paper as he went.

Friday had been marked up by him as the most likely date for the funerals and he was beginning to get his thoughts together. He knew that there would be more interest than usual for a funeral in the village. This would be very different. John Akehurst had many friends around about, while his contacts in the profession had been extensive. It was likely that many of those would come to pay their last respects to him. Then of course there was Elizabeth too. She was well regarded and her many acquaintances would certainly be here. And so he busied himself, reading passages, determining what he might say, what he might suggest in due course to Eleanor Ayres as an Order of Service, and thinking through the arrangements he would have to make the following day with the gravedigger. He had agreed several years ago with John Akehurst that he would have a plot in the cemetery by the stone wall at the north end. It was there that John's wife had been buried and so it seemed only fitting that they should also be close at their rest. Given his changed domestic circumstances since then Father Bolland considered it appropriate for Elizabeth to be next to John at rest, and so a plot needed to be allocated in his plans for her too. By ten that evening he was beginning to feel tired. As he made his way out of the church, dimming each of the lanterns as he passed them, he couldn't help but reflect on the injustice that had been brought upon these two kind hearted parishioners. He felt saddened and more upset than he had ever been before in his life as he locked the church and hurriedly made his way back to his house.

Early the following day he walked over to see Eleanor Ayres. She had risen earlier than usual, disturbed by her thoughts as well as having Mary beside her in the bed. She had also been woken at around five by Will, who had slept in front of the hearth downstairs wrapped in only a blanket, and who had woken her when he had knocked over a chair during the night as he went outside to relieve himself.

She had prepared herself for Father Bolland's arrival and was expecting him as he approached the dwelling.

'Good morning Eleanor.'

'Morning. Good of you to come. Come inside. Would you like something to drink? I've got a lovely vegetable soup warming by the fire; can I get you some of that?'

'That will be lovely,' he said, settling himself and the papers he had brought with him carefully at the kitchen table. He sat quietly as she scooped some of the soup from the pot. She admonished herself as she spilt some of it on her hand. She cleaned it away with the hem of her pinafore.

'There you are. That should warm you.'

The back door opened and Mary and Will entered. They acknowledged him politely, but said nothing else, making their way across the room before sitting down. They sat looking at the hearth in a slightly detached manner, before Mary said,

'Why don't we leave you to it?'

'No. No. There's no need to go. You can stay and help me and Father Bolland'.

'I think we'll go and get some fresh air. Will?'

And with that she rose, collected their coats and with a cheery goodbye left.

The priest kept his counsel, but could not easily hide his disappointment and dismay at the way they seemed unconcerned and disinterested in supporting Eleanor.

'She's upset. Just trying not to show it really,' Eleanor said, when she could see what Father Bolland was thinking.

'Yes.' He paused for a second, 'I'm sure.'

Eleanor tried to mask her feelings at Mary's thoughtlessness, but her hands began to tremble and she could feel herself feeling dizzy. She turned away from his gaze for a second to gather herself, before looking at him again, cheerily.

'What do you think we should have as the opening hymn?' she said breezily.

'John loved this one,' he said starting to hum the tune aloud to her as he turned the opened page towards her.

She read the first verse, the tune running in her head as she did so.

'Yes, that'll be nice. And I know Elizabeth liked that one too.'

'And then I thought we might sing this one later,' he said, turning to a page he had marked with a slip of paper. Again as he allowed her time to read the verse he gently hummed the refrain. She smiled as he did so, and then joined in the chorus with him.

'That'll be fine,' she said, cheered by his company and attention.

'I've marked on these pages the three prayers that I would like to say between the hymns and before we move on into the more formal part of the service.' He again turned to a page that he had marked in one of the prayer books that he had brought with him.

He read the first prayer out aloud; paused for a few seconds at the end, before moving on to read the second passage. At his side Eleanor followed the text as he read. The tears were beginning to well up. Eventually she couldn't contain herself any longer and soon broke down in an uncontrollable flood of tears.

'There,' he said, putting his arm around her. 'It's a difficult time for you. But we'll get through it together. You'll see.'

They sat motionless for a while until she reached for a piece of linen she had tucked in her dress, which she used to dry her eyes.

'Yes. You're right,' she said as she got up and went over to the hearth, where she stood looking into the burning embers. 'You're right,' she said quietly again.

'Let's talk about the rest of the service,' she said, turning again to him, and giving him a gentle smile to show her gratitude for his kindness.

'Of course.'

They had been through the details of the service and the arrangements for the burial, when Mary and Will returned. As they came up the path he could see that their mood was carefree and that they were enjoying a joke together. Their attitude then was in stark contrast as they came inside the house, when they both became taciturn and sober.

'Well, I think we've covered most of what we can do today,' he said. 'I'll have a word with the funeral director and speak to the chief constable when I go into Leatherhead later this morning. But as far as I can see, it seems that we will be able to hold the service on Friday, in the early afternoon. Is that alright with you Eleanor?'

'Yes, father.'

'Fine. Then I had best be off. Good day to you. Good day Mary. Good day Will.' And collecting up his books swiftly he was away.

Eleanor didn't say anything once he had gone. She spooned and drank two ladles of soup, washed the cup that the priest had used, before making her way to the back of the dwelling, where she busied herself feeding the seven chickens she had in a pen there.

Mary and Will meantime sat themselves at the table. Each shrugged their shoulders silently at the other before breaking into a smile. They clasped hands and giggled again at the joke they had shared earlier.

*****

Father Bolland made his way to the blacksmith. He often borrowed a trap from the owner Thomas so that he could fulfil some of the obligations that he had outside the village. Thomas' business was well known in the area and frequented by most of the farmers in the surrounding district. With his lean frame and unpolished manner many thought him a difficult person to deal with, but the priest had never had a bad word to say against him and was grateful for his help.

'Good morning, Thomas,' he said, hesitating slightly at the gate leading into the yard so as not to offend. 'Is there any chance I could have the use of a trap today? I have to go down into Leatherhead shortly and didn't really want to walk there and back.'

Thomas stood in the yard, a large iron in his right hand. He didn't respond immediately, which had an unsettling effect on the priest, as if he were mentally calculating something difficult. Then his face showed the faintest glimmer of a frown, before he acknowledged Father Bolland's greeting and responded.

'Could be difficult just now; but in about an hour if you come back I'll have one set up for you. Mind you get back before dark though.'

'That's very kind of you, Thomas. An hour. Fine. And of course I'll be back in good time, before it gets dark.' He felt a little anxious, but hoped that this hadn't showed in his voice.

'Until later then. Goodbye. And thank you again.'

'No problem, father,' he heard as he turned and began to make his way to the church to busy himself.

The hour passed quickly enough and soon the priest found himself riding a trap down into Leatherhead. He took the opportunity to call in to see a friend, who lived just outside the town, and whose house he passed on the way. Staying for a short time, only too aware of Thomas' warning, it wasn't long before he was tying the horse in the yard at Union Hall.

The desk officer greeted him with a polite 'Sir' in acknowledgement of his arrival, and then asked,

'What can I do for you today, sir?'

Having explained that he would like to speak to the chief constable about the release of John Akehurst's and Elizabeth Haines' bodies for burial, the officer went off to enquire. As the priest waited he casually watched the various comings and goings in the yard until the officer returned.

'He'll be with you shortly, sir. Take a seat.'

'Thank you,' he replied, taking a seat opposite as instructed. He amused himself, thinking about the morning and turned his brimmed hat round and round in his fingers. Footsteps alerted him to the arrival at his side of the chief constable.

'Good morning, father. Come through.'

Turning quickly he made his way up the corridor, with the priest in hot pursuit.

'How can I help you?' he said having seated himself at his desk and offered, with a gesture, for his guest to be seated.

The priest explained that he needed to make the funeral arrangements for his two unfortunate parishioners and wanted now to establish when the burial arrangements could be made.

'Yes, I understand,' he said, rising and now pacing the floor to the left of Father Bolland, who followed his progress attentively.

'Yes,' he said again, seemingly to nobody in particular. And then he began to describe what action had been taken to find the killers and how so far this had given them no leads at all. He was clearly disturbed by this and his frustration, anger and real concern was not hidden too deep below the surface. The priest listened attentively. He didn't try and interrupt. Then suddenly the chief constable stopped, moved to his desk to pick up his pipe, lit it with a slim piece of wood retrieved from the fire, and then sitting once again opposite the priest he said:

'Yes. Of course. We mustn't delay what needs to be done. When were you planning the burials?'

'I had thought Friday.'

'Friday. Yes, that seems fine. Let me order the officer to make the arrangements. Would you like us to bring the bodies to your church?'

'It would be helpful if you could have John and Elizabeth brought back up to Bookham, but can I ask that you have them taken to the funeral director there? Can that be done in the morning?'

'Yes. Of course. I'll have the officer arrange that for you. Is there anything else I can help you with?'

'No; thank you. You have been most helpful.'

'Until later then,' he said showing Father Bolland to the door.

Returning to Bookham he called in to see Eleanor and informed her that her father and Elizabeth Haines would be brought back to the village in the morning and that Friday was being set as the day for the service. She was clearly pleased that he had been able to arrange that for her, kissing his hand three times to show her gratitude.

'Thank you, father,' she kept repeating.

'Where are the two youngsters?' he enquired as he stood at the front door ready to leave.

'Out,' she said slightly dismissively. 'Better things to do I expect.'

'Oh. Well you will be sure to let Mary know.'

And with that he was gone, back to Thomas' without delay before the light faded further.

—〰—

FIVE

By midday nearly all of the businesses in Bookham had closed their doors for the day. The anticipation of what was about to take place that afternoon was palpable. Even the dogs seemed to sense something in the air as they ran with apparent intent along the main street to settle quietly somewhere else, unobtrusive. The children at the school had been given that afternoon off and once the excitement of that treasured prize had been absorbed were chastened and taken soberly home by their mothers. The air was crisp, light and sharpened by a lukewarm sun that hung low to the south west of the village.

At two o'clock the large gates into the funeral director's yard were opened and the first hearse moved forward steadily. The sound of the eight recently shoed feet of the two mares scrapped on the gravel as they strained initially to pull the weight and then to make the turn left towards the church. The second hearse, which carried the body of Elizabeth Haines, followed closely. The driver of each hearse had on a black top coat, top hat, gloves, and a starched white shirt, set off with a large black tie, which had been generously bowed. Beside each sat a young apprentice. They looked pallid, their eyes intense with worry. They too had been dressed formally for the occasion, although their frail frames and awkwardness did not create the same sense of gravitas being displayed by their masters. Those in the street stopped and gazed, silent, heads slightly bowed, as the hearses passed them. As they reached the centre of the village the publican led a group out from the tavern, which initially kept quiet, but which soon were clapping to show their regard for the two.

The hearses crossed the road and entered the church precinct through the gates that had been held open for them. As these were shut the parishioners, who had been waiting on the grass either side of the entrance, silently, fell in behind the second hearse and walked slowly with it.

Father Bolland had placed himself ahead of the first hearse, accompanied by Eleanor Ayres, Mary Ayres and Will Page. As they walked towards the main door he read aloud passages from his prayer book. It took several minutes for the congregation to be seated, during which time the funeral director had each coffin taken from its hearse and then held shoulder high by six pallbearers. When the organist, instructed by the priest struck the first melancholy chord, they stepped crisply forward. The tread of their heavy boots on stone slabs at the entrance echoed and was heard by those within.

The two coffins arrived at the front of the church and were positioned side by side, each on a table, at the foot of the steps leading up to the altar. Once the pallbearers had made their exit to the left, Eleanor Ayres stepped forward and laid a single white lily on each coffin, touching her lips and then the foot of each as she left it. When she returned to her seat Mary Ayres, dressed in black and veiled, then stepped forward to lay a rose on each coffin. When she had done that she looked up to the altar, crossed herself, bowed her head gently, turned, and retook her seat.

Father Bolland had stationed himself in the pulpit and began the service by asking the congregation to kneel. They recited the Lord's Prayer together, and then the Creed, before he read carefully a prayer that he had written with Eleanor Ayres earlier that day. He then invited the congregation to sing the hymn Eleanor had chosen, and as they all rose, each reaching in front of them for their hymn book, the organist played loudly the introductory bars of the tune.

Their singing was hesitant at first, but with the help of the four men and ten boys that comprised the church's choir, together with the vocal leadership given by the priest, they soon warmed and even sang each of the three choruses with gusto. At the end they sat noisily, feeling somewhat less tense and even, dare it be said, rather pleased with themselves. They were led through a further series of prayers, before they rose once more to sing a final hymn. Then the priest said a few words to them, praising and commending the virtues of both John Akehurst and Elizabeth Haines, before he informed them that the two deceased would now be taken into the cemetery, where the burial and committal would follow at the gravesides.

The pallbearers returned and cautiously raised their charges to shoulder height, before turning and progressing towards the back of the church. As the second coffin passed the parishioners left their pews and followed. The path to the left of the church entrance traced itself towards a large oak tree, besides which two deep holes had been dug. The three men, who had worked in the chill air most of the previous day, stood aside against the far wall of the churchyard. Their shovels dug into the turf.

Father Bolland waited until the congregation had settled again, before he began the formal renditions, with which he was fluent and word perfect. He paused once this had been completed, before saying one final prayer, his hands extended so that he could touch the foot of both coffins as they lay on the ground above each trench. He indicated with a nod for the funeral director to have the coffins lowered, before he leant forward to offer Eleanor Ayres the box containing soil. She took off the smart leather glove she was wearing on her right hand, grabbed a handful of earth and dropped it onto the top of the coffin in which John Akehurst lay. She then reached in again, and with the same motion threw a handful of earth onto Elizabeth Haines' coffin. She mumbled a blessing to herself as she completed this act.

Mary Ayres stood beside her. Contained. Separate. When offered the box she was visibly overcome, her shoulders shook, and the sound of her sobbing unsettled everyone there. Eventually she was able to take a handful of soil and dropped some, first on Elizabeth Haines' coffin and then onto the coffin lid in which John Akehurst lay. As the dirt hit the lid it dislodged the rose perched there. It moved, and then dropped softly to the earth at the base of his coffin.

Eleanor Ayres placed her arms around Mary's waist, and led her gently away. The rest of the congregation stood impassive for several minutes, as the box was offered and passed from hand to hand.

The light faded. They dispersed quietly, and while the hearses were turned to make their way back to the yard, the gravediggers stretched, collected their shovels and moved silently across the cemetery.

*****

A robin perched itself on a headstone. As Eleanor Ayres approached the gravesides the next Easter it darted first to another closer to her and then onto the headstone which marked John Akehurst's grave. It looked at her with a dark questioning eye before flying off into the security of a neighbouring tree. Eleanor had noticed its attention and smiled to herself. She leant down and picked up the flowers that now lay dry, brown and curled at the base of the headstone. With her gloved hands she scraped the soil on the grave to give it a fresher look, before she placed the six daffodils that she had picked as she came to church that morning. She said a few quiet words and then moved across to the grave of Elizabeth Haines, where she again removed the flowers that she had laid there last week and replaced them with daffodils. Behind her she could hear the chatter of parishioners still lingering at the church entrance after the Easter service. The choir sang one last chorus of the hymn that they had soloed earlier. The beauty of that hung gently in the crisp dry spring air.

Eleanor had found some peace since that terrible day in October last and her life had returned since to greater normality. Her days were spent sewing and tending to the fabrics on the large estate, where she had happily further enhanced her reputation as a seamstress. Her concern now was, unfortunately, centred on Mary. Eleanor had been left the cottage in her father John Akehurst's will, but in her kindness she had permitted Mary to live there since the start of the year. It seemed a sensible arrangement for her to be there, and anyway she had become rather attached to her own home and did not really want to have to move across the village. So that is how it had been settled.

Mary was clearly delighted to have her own place and couldn't thank her mother enough. But it seemed that her kindness was very soon forgotten and during the past few weeks she had become upset and concerned about the way that she was behaving. It didn't help either that others in the village had noted that too, and had made comments about it to her. That hurt.

Once Mary had moved into the cottage it wasn't long before Will had joined her. Perhaps naively, Eleanor now reflected, she hadn't appreciated the strength of their relationship, and certainly hadn't expected Mary to bring shame on her in this way. Their arrangement was compounded only weeks later when Will moved his mother and father into the cottage. Eleanor was surprised that Mary had allowed this, but as the weeks passed it became increasingly evident to her that her daughter had fallen under their spell. She was obviously besotted with Will, and reason wasn't going to stop her bringing opprobrium upon herself and her family.

ALAN DAWSON

The cottage had always been a thing of beauty. In July each year its front garden was filled with summer blooms, the beds tended and neat. Inside the rooms were immaculately clean, floors scrubbed, furniture polished, fireplace tended with care. The crockery that John and Elizabeth had acquired during their life was really quite exquisite and had been their pride. Elizabeth would ensure that it was kept pristine and where she could display pieces she did so. It gave her and John a good deal of pleasure. The contrast that Easter was stark. The cottage had become dirty and dishevelled. The floors had become covered in mud and other matter, which the four of them had casually brought into the cottage. Much of the furniture had now been stained and several chairs had had their wooden backs snapped, so that bits hung limply off them. The crockery had been used carelessly and now lay, dirty, in uneven heaps at one end of the kitchen. Outside the garden had overgrown and was a place where items not needed were simply discarded.

But it wasn't just their cavalier and unthinking actions that were so upsetting. Mary's general manner in particular had become a real worry. Where she had been a caring and gentle child, and Will an unassuming man, they now both appeared to behave in a way that displayed a distinct lack of concern about anyone else but themselves. They had become extremely self centred and selfish. When she visited them they were generally sullen and Will had very little to say to her at all. Will's parents were no better, treating the place as if they owned it and Eleanor as an unwelcome passer-by. While out in the village Will and his father, who frequented the tavern most of his waking hours, were seen to be brazen and loud. The language they were often heard to use was shocking. Mary meanwhile followed them everywhere, most of the time mute and submissive, but increasingly more outspoken and disruptive.

Their neighbours very quickly had become alarmed and had soon expressed their concerns not only to her but also to Father Bolland. He had seen the change for himself when he had visited the cottage a week or two before Easter, and he had taken Eleanor aside that same weekend when she attended the Sunday service. She was pleased that his manner had not been judgemental, but he had expressed his concern as if he were a disappointed uncle watching a beloved and favourite niece fall from grace. That was a comfort to her for relationships with some in the village had become noticeably more difficult. At least in him, she had thought to herself, she had a constant friend.

As she knelt by the graves she heard behind someone approaching up the path. She stood up and turning saw Father Bolland. He smiled and greeted her warmly and then as he put his hand gently on her shoulder spoke softly.

'I was in the town yesterday and had chance to meet the chief constable there. He wanted you to know that while progress was proving difficult they think that they have had a break through. They are questioning a man they brought in on Friday. It seems that he had on him an article, which went missing from John's cottage. He said that he would let me know if there is any positive development from that. At least it's some progress.'

'Thank you for letting me know that. It does seem to have taken so long that I was beginning to think that they had given up quite honestly.'

'No. No. I don't think that they'll ever do that,' he said, trying to reassure her.

'Anyway, I thought you would be pleased to know that. I'll leave you now,' he added.

He smiled, squeezed her shoulder touchingly, and turned to make his way back up the path before disappearing into the church.

She stood looking at the field over the wall at the top of the cemetery. Her thoughts with her father. She looked down to the graves again, and seeing something not quite in place on Elizabeth's grave, moved her left foot to and fro to straighten things up. She bowed her head, crossed herself and then turned to make her way home. At that moment she felt alone and rather lonely.

*****

The chief constable was beginning to get annoyed with his superintendent. It had been twenty four hours since the man had been detained in Dorking carrying the timepiece, which Robert Hall had noted was taken from the body of John Akehurst. It was a fine piece and one of which John was especially proud. He wore it every day with his jacket. The chief constable fingered it in his hand, running his thumb across its sleek glass cover and gold surround. He raised it to his ear and listened as the mechanisms inside clicked and turned. Time passed. He turned and glared at the superintendent, who stood to attention the other side of his desk.

'So he still hasn't told you where he came into possession of this watch; and you still don't know who sold it to him?'

'No, sir.'

'Well I think we had better persuade the young man. See to it and let me know when he does inform you.'

'Sir.'

Once he had left the room, the chief constable relaxed and looked at the face of the watch again. He thought what a delightful piece it was. However, he couldn't forget that he needed to use this evidence to progress the case. With so little progress having been made since the autumn, his competency to handle this double murder investigation was beginning to be questioned. He didn't like that at all, and his mood reflected that sentiment sorely. Certainly, he mused, he was not going to let some misfit in the cell below him stand in his way.

The methods his officers used to persuade the man were not pleasant. The twenty four year old, who was being subjected to their attention, had not felt pain that intense ever. He had had his right arm nearly broken behind his back, and his left thumb was completely numb from the pressure that they had put it under with the clamp that they had applied to it. He didn't think it clever much longer to not tell them what they needed to know. 'What was the point in not telling them?' he thought. All he had done was bought a stolen watch. 'What was the harm in that?' So as not to prolong his discomfort any further, looking at the superintendent, who was stood in the corner while his men worked him over, he said:

'Alright. Alright. Enough. I'll tell you what you want,' he pleaded.

The two officers relaxed their grip on his arms and shoulders and they too looked towards the superintendent.

'Right,' he said, signalling with a wave of his right hand for the officers to step back. 'Right. Tell me.'

'I got it off Will the cobbler.'

'Who?'

'Will Page.'

'Where?'

'In Dorking. Late last year. He offered it to me in a tavern there?'

'Which?'

'The White Horse.'

'Go on.'

'I gave him a shilling for it.'

'When?'

'I don't know.'

'You had better remember then,' the superintendent snarled, beckoning the two officers back to the prisoner.

'Last year. In October I think.' He paused. Looked to the floor for inspiration, but all he could see there was his own sweat. He looked to the wall, and then said:

'Yes it was October. We had just finished a fair in Westcott and I walked with him into Dorking. We had a drink or two at the White Horse, when he showed me the watch he had hidden at the bottom of his bag. The Westcott fair is near the end of the month I think.'

'Good. Very good. And where is your friend Will Page now?'

'Last time I saw him he was on his way to West Humble. But I think he's in Bookham these days. Can't be sure mind you.'

'Good. Very good,' the superintendent repeated.

'Let him have something to eat and drink,' he instructed his men as he opened the cell door and made his way upstairs.

When he entered the chief constable's office he was stood looking out of the window, pipe in hand. The chief constable turned.

'Seems that he bought the watch from a Will Page. A cobbler. Got it off him in Dorking last October. Probably at the end of that month. He thinks this Will Page lives in Bookham now, but he isn't certain. I'll have the constable there contacted immediately. He's likely to know if anyone does.'

The chief constable looked at the watch now sat prominently on his desk. He picked it up and ran his thumb across it again.

'Well done. Let me know when you've found him.'

'Yes, sir.'

Anxious to make the break through that they so needed the superintendent informed the desk officer that he was away to see constable Hall, and having had a horse saddled, rode with pace up the hill towards Bookham. Robert Hall had just enjoyed a large dinner, which his wife had cooked for them both on Easter Sunday afternoon, when the superintendent appeared outside. Once inside and after exchanging a few pleasantries with Robert Hall's wife, they went to his police office and the superintendent told him about their lead.

'Oh, him. Yes I know him. But this is going to surprise you. He's actually now living in John Akehurst's cottage in the village, down the road. Seems he and John's granddaughter Mary are living there together, and that his father and mother are there too. His father's made himself well known in the village. Loud and abusive, especially after the turn out from the tavern.'

'Good man. We had better go and find this Will Page then.

—◊—

SIX

The cart jolted forward and its occupants wrestled to regain their balance. They looked at each other and burst into cackles of laughter, deriding one another for being so inept. Spirits were high. Their day had been a long one, up since before dawn, but it all seemed to go well and the master was pleased. He had indeed taken the unusual step of coming to the back of the house, as they were all settling themselves, so that he could wish them well and thank them for their efforts over the Easter weekend. They had acknowledged his courtesy politely, and smiled weakly at him. They soon were relaxed again once he had headed off through the rose garden that bordered that part of the house.

The house was substantial. Built originally by John Mullay's grandfather about eighty years earlier it enjoyed a prominent and yet securely isolated position with its frontage looking south towards Leith Hill. Its fine portico was made of Portland stone and its external walls now enjoyed ample covering from plants, which had been planted by his father. In the summer they bloomed wonderfully filling the air with a range of exotic scents. The windows, opened wide along both sides of the house captured these, and the fragrances drifted inside, offering a charming surprise to any guest.

The Easter weekend gathering had been a tradition within John Mullay's family for at least a generation. Most of them had descended on the house in the week leading up to it, and then invited guests generally arrived on the Saturday. That day was usually spent enjoying a light lunch, settling into the fine accommodation that had been allocated, and was then followed by a formal dinner in the evening. At the end of the dinner the ladies would withdraw to the large lounge in the west wing of the house, while the gentleman enjoyed cigars and port, before moving to the card room. The gentle chatter in the former contrasted vividly with the mirth that emanated from there. By around one o'clock the guests had had enough and each made their way respectfully to bed.

Breakfast on the Easter Sunday, as on most Sundays in reality, was taken at leisure in the informal dining room. There a buffet of hot and cold dishes had been laid out carefully by the domestic staff so that the guests were able to graze from it. First editions of newspapers from Fleet Street had been brought from the stagecoach relay stop at Ripley at dawn that morning. The clanking of cutlery on fine bone china and the rustle of papers being turned was the dominant sound for much of the first part of the morning.

At eleven o'clock traditionally the guests would go to the chapel. This year the Bishop of Guildford was one of the guests and he had agreed to lead their own Easter Sunday service. The chapel stood about a furlong away in the grounds. Just before eleven all of the guests and the family, some twenty people, had made their way up the gravelled path leading to it.

The service was shortened on this occasion, and it was clear from the smiles on all of their faces as they returned that they had enjoyed it.

Lunch was taken precisely at one o'clock and was announced by the head butler, who gave a single hammer blow to the large gong that stood in the entrance hall. Its bass tone resonated throughout the house for several seconds and brought the guests quickly to the principal dining room situated off the entrance hall, where they had dined the previous evening.

The large table, covered in fine linen, was beautifully decorated, with the lit chandeliers above creating a warm and welcoming atmosphere once again. The bishop, who was seated next to his host at the head of the table, said grace. They all then settled. Whereas the previous evening's conversations had been sporadic, fairly exact and polite, the guests, who were now more familiar and comfortable with each other, soon fell into more casual banter. Light hearted laughter and chatter quickly filled the room. They enjoyed a four course lunch, all of the ingredients for which had been grown on the estate. John Mullay was proud of that and during the lunch he made a point of letting his guests know. Someone to his left rattled their cutlery on the table in approval, and everyone followed his lead.

Carriages had been arranged at four o'clock, and by four thirty the estate was once again tranquil. The peacocks could be heard sounding off in the walled garden, while below the long walk that led away to the west of the house, the young lambs could be heard bleating for their supper.

John Mullay was a good host and enjoyed the company of others. He also enjoyed displaying his wealth. His real interest was, however, in commerce, and while he had mixed freely with his guests he had with intention singled out one individual, with whom he wanted to discuss his business dealings. He had known Sir Roland since childhood. Indeed both as youngsters had once enjoyed a private tutelage together at a school near their London homes in Mayfair, before he went up to Eton College. Both had inherited wealth, but had followed different paths. Sir Roland had initially studied commercial law before becoming a banker. John Mullay, always a more confident, independent and restless child, had used the opportunity that his wealth had afforded him to develop extensive interests in the Caribbean. There he had settled for eight years as a young man and had in that time created a large plantation, where he grew tobacco and sugar cane. The plantation had been developed through the use of slave labour shipped in from West Africa. That was at the beginning. Times had since changed. He was now experiencing difficulty in finding and controlling labour on the plantation and needed to get advice on what he might do about it from his friend. They had discussed it fully, but had not been able to conclude what the correct course of action might be. Sir Roland agreed that he would think more about it and be in touch with his friend very soon once he had sounded out some of his contacts in London.

With the house now peaceful John Mullay eased himself into a comfortable chair in his first floor study. From his window he could see the pale pink sky as the sun began to set. He downed in one the whisky that he had just poured. A good weekend he thought to himself. And yet, not quite complete. He stood, felt excited, and set off towards the stairs that led to the head housekeeper's quarters. He knocked gently on the wooden door and heard her footsteps approaching. She opened the door and gave him a broad, welcoming smile. She had been expecting him to visit her and she had readied herself. They had been lovers for just over five years now, had become good friends and close companions. Nevertheless they continued to shroud their relationship from others, although they were never quite certain how successful they had been at doing that. She was sure that some of her staff were aware, but nobody had to date mentioned it to her directly, and she had not seen any sign in the way they behaved to indicate that anyone knew.

Her room, small and high up in the west wing, was beautifully kept. There were two narrow windows that allowed the fading light to brighten the room and on the window sills she had plants, that were beginning to bloom. Besides a chair that she had covered in a bright, soft fabric and placed close to the fireplace, there was a dark wood table and two wooden chairs. Against one wall she had her bed. The linens were exquisite, albeit that they were actually rejects from one of the guest bedrooms, which she had restored earlier that year.

'You look wonderful,' he said, stepping inside.

She closed the door softly, listening for the sound of the click as she did so. Although nobody actually ventured up to her room, they had no reason ever to do so, she still turned the key in the lock to ensure their privacy.

'It's been a wonderful weekend and the guests seemed to enjoy themselves.' She paused for a while, touched his cheek, and then added, 'that bishop's a saucy one. You should have seen what he tried to do with me when we passed in the corridor this morning!'

He smiled, loving her way, before he moved towards her and they dropped onto the bed. They embraced with passion.

Later as she fussed about rearranging herself, he stood looking out of one of the windows. It was now quite dark.

'I'm off to the West Indies later this week,' he said casually.

'Oh,' she said, trying not to show that she was upset that he would be away from her for at least two months.

'It's sometime since I've been over there and it needs my attention before it ruins me. I really hate leaving you, and the house. But it must be done.'

They settled again, propped up together on her bed.

He had not married, and did not have any children. So he reflected, as they lay there watching the flame flick and lick the back of the hearth, at least he was spared the pain of separation that some of his friends had on their long passages overseas.

They embraced each other tenderly and lay quietly for sometime, until her left arm became numb from where he had rested on her. As she pulled it away from underneath him, he woke. The room was very much darker and now quite cold, the fire having retreated to dull embers. She got up and lit a lamp, and that prompted him to gather himself.

'I'd better be away. I'll come and see you again before I leave, my love.'

He kissed her softly. Unlocking the door, he turned to take another look at her beautiful face before he left, trying to make as little noise as possible as he descended her staircase.

He didn't get to see her again before he had to go, but wrote her a note, which he placed carefully under her door. His plans had been disrupted by the arrival of a carriage driven up from Portsmouth early the next morning. The driver announced that the captain of the merchant ship, on which he was sailing, was now leaving on the late tide that day, two days earlier than he had expected. He cussed at the news, but hurriedly had his things packed for the voyage, and by midday he and his personal aide were headed on the trail along the Hog's Back towards Portsmouth.

He had sailed on this merchant ship before. It was cramped and dirty, but he knew that it was reliable and that the captain could be trusted. On board he was shown where he was to be accommodated by a young hand, who was probably no older than twelve. The captain's cabin at the stern was through a door close to his accommodation. He had been allocated the starboard side to help shelter him from the sun, which would soon become fierce as they travelled south towards the Azores. He had a bunk, slim and raised, below which he could stow his clothes and papers. Although housed on an open deck, he was able to gain some privacy from the two officers who shared that same area, by drawing a curtain across. But he soon found that this made everything stuffy and claustrophobic, and so rapidly he became used to sharing his life in the close company of others.

The merchant ship had been loaded by dusk that day and as the tide rose they cast off and made their way out into the channel. The sea was at first calm and he took the opportunity of the mild weather to go on deck. As he stood alone below the wheel, he could see the lights on shore, surprisingly bright at first, but soon just distant and dull. By eight thirty they were sailing south west in a tar black sea. He shivered as the wind swept across the large sails above him. He felt excited. Another journey. An adventure. But he also felt for the first time in his life that he would rather have been at home this minute with his girl. He looked into the sea, which was now churning softly below him, and then carefully made his way back to his bunk. He lay there, eyes closed, with a heavy heart.

His first night on board was fitful. The two officers, with whom he was sharing, interrupted his sleep throughout the night either with their incessant banter, or simply in making their four hours watch changeovers. By daybreak he had had enough and rolled himself off his bunk, landing heavily on the deck. The noise ironically awoke the officer, who only half an hour ago had crept into his bunk for a final sleep, and who now appeared to let out an anguished cry of despair beneath his covers at being drawn back into some form of consciousness. John Mullay grinned and then made his way to the main deck. As he came out into the early morning light he turned and acknowledged the other officer, who was stood at the wheel, looking frozen. The sea ahead was dark and threatening, while behind was a stream of white where the ship had just cut its path. As the sun rose over the horizon the ship's passage was illuminated with a yellow hue. He paused to stare at its beauty for a while. Then he began to notice the smell. It rose up below his feet and was as pungent an odour as he had ever smelt before. Stepping forward towards the latticed hatches that were set around the deck he peered below and saw in the dark beneath his feet cattle, pigs and sheep. They were tightly packed together in a series of pens. At first they were unsettled by his movement above them. Turning away John Mullay drew in a large mouthful of air to rid himself of the stench that now seemed to have been drawn into his being. Recovered, he returned to his bunk and lay still, overcome with nausea. This was going to be a long passage he thought to himself.

—〰—

SEVEN

They didn't find Will Page at the cottage. There was a light inside the front room indicating that someone was at home, but there was no obvious sign of any activity. They knocked twice. Nobody came to answer. They decided to go around the back to see if they would have better luck there. In the back garden they found Will Page's father defecating close to the hedge. He acknowledged their arrival as they quickly stopped in their tracks and retreated back into the lane, where they stood patiently listening to his movements. After what seemed an age, he called to them:

'What can I do for you two gentlemen?'

They stepped forward, declining to shake the hand he proffered them as graciously as they were able to muster.

'We would like to speak to Will Page. Is he here?'

'What's he done now?'

'Where is he?'

'What's the problem?' he replied, his tone now beginning to sound more offensive than at first.

'No problem. We just want to ask him some questions. Where is he?'

'Well he isn't here. He's been away for several days now. Doing some fairs near London I think.'

'When do you expect him back?'

'Can't say I know.'

'Well if you see him, can you ask him to come and see the constable at the police house immediately.'

'Right,' he said, unconvincingly. 'Right,' he said again as if to emphasise his enthusiasm and commitment.

'Thank you. Good evening to you.'

That was three months ago. Will Page had not been seen since that time. At Union Hall the superintendent was still regularly being questioned about what steps he was taking to apprehend the man, but as the days passed less and less progress was actually made. The case seemed to be quietly being forgotten.

Along a quiet track about a mile outside Oxshott two figures approached the police officer, who had at that moment stopped to allow his horse time to drink from the puddle. He watched as they came slowly closer to him, ambling rather than walking, chatting to each other, apparently oblivious of his presence ahead of them. The officer could see that one was a slim, dark haired women aged in her early twenties, while the other was a tall, athletic young man. Even from that distance he could see that they looked tired and dishevelled. The hem of the girl's dress was soaked, while the tunic he wore was muddied and sodden. Over his right shoulder he was carrying a large canvas bag. It was evidently heavy and uncomfortable as it cut into him. The horse raised its head from the puddle and whinnied. The noise made them look up and they were surprised to see someone else here so early in the morning. The officer continued to watch them attentively as they came closer to him. As they drew to his side he put out his hand

'Where are you two off to at this time of day?'

'Back to Bookham.'

'Do you live there?'

'Yes.'

'Where have you come from?'

'Been walking since dawn from Kingston.'

'What were you doing there?'

'There's been a market there this week and we've been selling.'

'What's your business?'

'She's a painter. I'm a cobbler?'

'What are your names?'

'What's with all these questions officer?'

'Just answer the question. What are your names?'

'I'm Will Page. This is Mary Ayres.'

'What have you got in that bag?'

'Tools for my business. Knives, leather. That sort of thing.'

'Let me see.'

Will obliged by dropping the bag to the ground and opening it widely so that the officer could see the contents. The officer stepped forward and peered into the bag. He reached down and pointed at a particular item that lay along its length.

'What's that?'

'A stretcher. I use it for stretching leathers.'

'Let me see it?'

The piece weighed heavily as the officer took it off Will. He looked it up and down, admiring the tool.

'So you use this to stretch leathers,' he said to nobody in particular. 'Why the two sharp metal bits here?'

Will gave him an explanation, to which the officer seemed to be only half interested in listening. He handed the piece back to Will and then started to thumb through a black covered notebook that he took from a pocket inside his tunic.

The two of them stood there, waiting for the officer to say something as he flicked through the pages. Will stowed the piece back inside his bag and drew it up to his shoulder as if to make on their way again, when the officer stopped on a page and read its contents to himself carefully once, and then again.

He looked up, stared at them both for a second or two before he said:

'You're Will Page you say?'

'Yes.'

'Well Will I want you to come with me now to my police house at Oxshott. There are some things I need to ask you there.'

'What?'

'Come with me and we'll talk when we get there.'

Mary by now was beginning to shiver. It was probably the cold, but she knew that she was frightened. She just hoped that Will was going to be sensible. Taking his elbow she said calmly,

'Come on Will, better do what the officer is asking.'

He looked at her. He sensed that she was frightened. He gave her a kind smile and then indicated to the officer that they would follow him.

He let them walk ahead as he rode his horse behind them. He couldn't help but notice how attached each was to the other, and he was rather touched as he watched them holding hands and leaning into each other as they ambled along.

It took the rest of the day for a rider to get across to Union Hall and return with officers and a wagon. Will had been advised that he was wanted for questioning there, and one would have thought that he might have been curious to know why. But his curiosity didn't get the better of him and he simply sat in a room adjoining the officer's with Mary. They spoke only occasionally. For much of the time he had his eyes fixed on the floor in front of him, his feet shuffling intermittently from side to side, which made an annoying scraping sound. Mary sat at his side, hands resting on her lap. As the morning progressed to afternoon they were given some food and she was advised to continue her journey before it got dark again. She resisted the advice, not at first seeming to understand that she was going to be alone once Will was taken away to Union Hall. After the officer had suggested for the third time that she be on her way, he could hear them discussing their situation in whispers, and then some ten minutes later Mary collected what little she had with her, gave Will a kiss and a hug, and tearfully left the police house.

As she walked out of Oxshott she saw the police wagon arriving from Union Hall, and about half an hour later, as she was sat at the side of the road dislodging a stone, which had become trapped inside the lining of her right shoe, it rattled passed her again at speed. There were two officers up front and a third in the back. He was sat next to Will, who as they passed her raised a hand to greet her. It was then that she saw that he was now manacled. She was shocked and it took her more time than she had to return his wave, by which time the wagon had started to descend rapidly downwards away from the brow of the hill. She stood up, waved her hands and blew him a kiss, but by then he had turned and missed it all. She watched the wagon until it reached the base of the hill, disappearing out of her sight when it turned sharp left towards Leatherhead. She now felt more alone than she had ever felt in her life.

*****

'Well Will, why don't you tell me about how you came to have this in your possession?' As he finished the question the superintendent placed the watch on the table where Will was sat. Not replying straight away he just looked at the piece opened before him and noted that it was now just after seven o'clock.

'What do you mean?'

'Come on Will. You had this in your possession and you sold it on. Why don't you tell me about it?'

The line of questioning went on for another half an hour without any progress being made. The superintendent was not certain at that stage whether he was dealing with an innocent here or a cunning thief. When he had taken time to relieve himself and to find a drink, he returned with the bag that Will had been carrying.

'This lot yours?' he said, as he dumped it without ceremony on the hard floor.

'Yes,' Will said taking a cursory glance downwards.

'Perhaps you could take everything out of it and we'll see what you have in there. It'll make a change for us all,' he said, trying not to be overly sarcastic.

Will leant forward, drew the bag between his feet, and began to take the items one by one from it. He laid them on the floor beside him. Towards the bottom of the bag lay the stretcher, which now had wedged itself in tightly, so that he could not immediately extricate it. Eventually it released and he pulled it out. As he was about to lay it alongside his other tools, the superintendent moved off the wall against which he had been leaning as he nonchalantly watched everything.

'That's an interesting piece. What do you use that for?' he said, as he snatched it from Will's grasp.

Will explained how he used it as the superintendent walked softly up and down the room, eyeing the tool and turning it over in his hands as he did so. He noted the two sharp metal bits at one end of the tool. Standing over Will, so that he had to crane his neck to look at him, the superintendent asked:

'And how long have you had this tool?'

'Since the end of last year.'

'And where did you get it?'

'Off a man in Dorking.'

'Who?'

'I only met him the once. He came to my stall at the market there and offered it to me. Hadn't a good one then, which was a bit of a problem, and he wasn't asking much for it, so I took it off him.'

'Really?'

'Yes.'

'So you can recall that. So then Will,' he said his tone now menacing. 'Now let's go back and see what you can remember about the watch.'

The superintendent kept at him for at least another hour, before he turned, looked at the officer stood by the door and said:

'Take him down. We'll finish with this in the morning,' and he took one glowering look at Will before he left the room, his boots echoing in the passage outside as he strode purposefully away.

*****

He hadn't made the connection at first. Then at dawn as he lay restlessly beside his wife, she oblivious to the world and snoring like a pup with a wheeze, he realised. He got up, put on a robe, and went into the adjoining room, where he had a writing desk that he used occasionally to finish off his paperwork. He flicked through the papers sat there until he came across the police doctor's report. He read the words to himself, three times.

'Each victim had two distinct puncture wounds to the back of their skull.'

'Distinct puncture wounds,' he repeated yet again as he carefully replaced the papers back into the folio.

The chief constable was late that morning, delayed by a visit he had to make to the dentist to have a tooth that had irritated him for weeks fixed. He looked pale when the superintendent got to see him around eleven o'clock that day. They didn't share much small talk; their relationship had become more strained in the past month, and so the superintendent was very soon able to explain to him what had happened in the last twenty four hours, and for him to hear the superintendent's startling request.

'And so what I am proposing, sir, is that we have the body of John Akehurst and of Elizabeth Haines disinterred so that we can determine precisely if this tool might be the murder weapon.'

Shocked, he didn't give him an immediate positive response. He was only too well aware of the sensitivities involved in such an undertaking, but also understood very clearly that they had up until now made no progress whatsoever in apprehending the criminal or criminals, who had carried out the dreadful crime. Acutely he knew that his future career prospects were now less rosy than they had been a year earlier. And so, with some reluctance, which was reflected in the tone of his voice eventually he responded.

'Fine. Speak to the priest and have it arranged for this evening at ten o'clock. No fanfares, please. Let's keep this very quiet. And make sure that those gravediggers don't talk about it. I'll join you there at ten.'

'Sir.'

The superintendent could hardly contain himself as he left the office. He summoned one of his most trusted officers, told him what was to be arranged, instructed that Will Page be retained until tomorrow for questioning, before he set off to Bookham to speak to Father Bolland.

*****

Guy Soden had been hanging around Union Hall for the past two and a half hours. As a local reporter and occasional correspondent for several of the Fleet Street newspapers, he was well known. Most simply sought to avoid him. His manner was intrusive as one might expect. Guy Soden was more than that. He could be obnoxious and self serving, with little interest in others. Only concerned about impressing himself and his editors. He was at Union Hall that day to find out more about some rustling that had been worrying his readers in the past month. He couldn't help notice that his old friend Will Page was being detained in the cells and that he had now been there, according to the desk officer, whom he had flattered incessantly to finally obtain the information, for over a day. His attention turned from rustling to the murders in Bookham, when he inadvertently overheard a conversation that the superintendent was having in the yard with one of his colleagues as Guy Soden lingered at the back of a trap that was parked there. It wasn't obvious to him at first what was being said. His instinct, nevertheless, soon told him that there had been some kind of breakthrough in the case. The superintendent's revived hyperactivity alone told its own story. His suspicions were confirmed when the superintendent took one of the traps and rode off with another officer towards Bookham. It took him an effort to follow them, but doing so was to prove worthwhile. Once they had tracked down Father Bolland, whose shock at what was being suggested was a joy for Guy Soden to watch, their supposedly casual stroll towards the church to the graves of John Akehurst and Elizabeth Haines had him panting with excitement. He watched from the street, peering through a small gap, which he had further enlarged, in the dry stone wall.

The superintendent and Father Bolland stood over the graves for several minutes. The cleric gesturing frantically, and then eventually taking a seat close by, where he sat with his head on his hands, which by now were visibly shaking. The superintendent followed him over to the seat and sat, stiffly, at his side. Nothing was said between them for a while, and then when the priest looked up he seemed to have reconciled himself to the task ahead, and once again became animated. It was then that the leading gravedigger appeared from the other side of the church. Heavily built he carried with him a large spade, which he held as if it were made of balsa wood. Before he got to the two of them, he rested the spade against the border wall, and then approached them, hands in pockets.

The gravedigger listened as Father Bolland explained what needed to be done that night, turning occasionally to the superintendent as if to reinforce one of the points he was making. The superintendent sat still, but nodded frequently, as the priest spoke. There was little if any reaction from the gravedigger either during the monologue or when it had finished. As if to ensure that the gravedigger had understood what was required of him the superintendent then reinforced some of the remarks that the priest had just made. The gravedigger nodded and then made off in the direction from which he had come, collecting his spade as he walked passed it. Little else was said between the two men as they rose and walked pensively to the west gate, where the second officer had been stood holding the horse's reins. They said their goodbyes and the two officers headed towards the police house. Father Bolland made his way into the church. He needed to check passages to deal correctly with tonight's event. By now he was feeling flustered and out of sorts. He hoped that its sanctuary and work would settle him.

Guy Soden thought that his presence hadn't been noted, but not much got passed the landlady at the tavern. From a small window at the top of the building she had seen him stood there, and had watched as the superintendent and the priest spoke. She had even seen the gravedigger arrive and the several gestures that were made towards the graves, above which they had first stood. It really didn't take much to make some apparent sense of what might be going on there. The reporter's presence merely reinforced her suspicions.

Within five minutes of her returning to the bar the news was out, much to the chagrin of Guy Soden, who thought he would spend the rest of the day quietly in the comfort of the hostelry secretly coddling his scoop. Listening to the incessant speculation and chatter got to him within the first hour. As he finished his tankard and took a final bite from the indigestible pie that he had played with as he sat there, he hit upon the idea of going to see if he could get a story from another angle. He made his way across the street and moved swiftly down past the church towards the cottage. He had heard from locals that Mary Ayres now lived there and that she had Will Page's parents living there too. It hadn't passed his notice that their behaviour since arriving had upset many of the villagers, and that Mary's manner was not what it used to be. He was intrigued and was looking forward to meeting her.

The cottage certainly looked lived in. The door was wide open and he simply announced himself to whoever might be there and stepped inside. He called again. There was no response. Confidently, and somewhat arrogantly, he walked through the cottage, viewing items as he strolled by them, occasionally picking up something that caught his particular attention. He placed items back casually, not really caring if he had moved them from their original position. Then he heard movement above him and heavy footsteps descending the wooden stair. Moving quickly to the front of the cottage to recover his position he was confronted head on by a large, unkempt middle aged man, who was still adjusting his clothing as they met.

'Who the hell are you?' he bellowed.

'My name's Guy Soden. I'm a reporter.'

'And what the hell do you think you're playing at here?'

'Well,' he hesitated, 'well, I was looking for Mary Ayres?'

'She's not here. What do you want with her anyway?'

'I wanted to speak to her about Will Page?'

'What about him?' he said aggressively, and as he did he moved even closer. Guy could now smell his body odour and breathe, but he tried not to antagonise the man further by smarting at it.

'Well he's being held in Union Hall, and...,' before he could finish his sentence the man retorted viciously:

'She knows that. What about it?'

'Well,' and he couldn't at that point stop himself, 'well, they're going to dig up the two bodies soon.'

As he said it he wished he hadn't, but consoled himself by knowing that the man would have probably found out for himself shortly once he got himself into the tavern again.

'What? What the hell did you just say?'

'They're going to dig up the bodies in the graveyard?'

'Who?'

'The police. I've just seen them arranging things with the priest. They must be onto something.'

'Get out,' he snarled, pushing him out of the front door.

He stumbled as he turned and fell to the ground. The man then kicked him hard in the back as he lay there.

'You bastard,' he shouted as he got up and made his way as quick as he could to the street. 'You stupid, ignorant bastard.'

The pain started to ease as he made his way towards the village, but cleared instantly when he caught sight of Mary Ayres as she crossed at the junction. She was carrying a wicker basket laden with bread and vegetables. He moved towards her hastily and stopped her as she was nearing the entrance to the church.

'Mary.'

She looked up, hesitated for a second, but not recognising the man, made to pass him.

He grabbed her arm and again called her name, adding as he did so:

'I'm a friend of Will. I'm Guy Soden.'

She stared at him blankly, then gave him a curt acknowledgement, before trying to move away and have him release her.

'I'm a friend of Will. I know he's at Union Hall. You must be very concerned?'

She didn't answer immediately. She stood her ground, and as he sensed her do that he gently let go of her arm.

'Have you seen him?'

'Yes,' he lied.

'How was he?'

'He was fine. Shaken but fine. I don't know how long he's going to be down there though. There's something going on.' At that point he thought he would tell her about the graves.

'Don't be so foolish,' she immediately responded. 'They can't do that.'

'Well, as I said, I've seen the police here today and it seems clear to me that they're going to dig your grandfather up sometime very soon. They must be onto something,' he added, trying intentionally to provoke her a little. She simply stood there. Incredulous.

'I can't stand here listening to your stupid nonsense,' she said scornfully, and was just about to say something else to him when she caught sight of the priest leaving the church.

'Father. Father,' she shouted, immediately drawing his attention. He changed direction and headed down the adjoining path towards them.

'Well ask him then if you don't believe me,' Guy Soden shouted rather childishly, as she ran away from him, through the gate, her feet noisily moving the gravelled path.

He watched as they met. The priest initially looked shocked as she demanded to know from him what might be going on. He didn't have much option other to let her know the plan for that evening and Guy Soden could see the reaction that its confirmation had on her. What surprised him, and clearly the priest too, was the physical abuse she gave him, beating his arms furiously, all the while screaming profanities at him.

'Mary. Mary,' he shouted at her. 'Calm down. Now.'

His appeals made no difference and a few seconds later he simply walked away from her, leaving her shouting at the top of her voice as he retreated hastily towards the main gate of the church.

Guy Soden slipped through the gate that had been left ajar. He shut it carefully behind him and made his way slowly towards her. She had sat herself, sobbing, on a bench. He sat down but kept a little distance from her. He didn't say anything. Then as she wiped her eyes and appeared more in control he looked at her, gave her a kind smile, and took her hand in his.

'They're going to open the graves tonight.'

'Yes.'

'I really cannot believe it. What's the point of that? What really is the point of that?' she repeated to herself.

'I don't know. But they must have reason. It isn't something that's done every day. I'll try and find out for you.'

'Can you? Can you, please. And please see if you can find out what they're up to with Will?'

'I'll try.'

They sat there and he began to ask her innocently about herself, her family, Will's parents. She was very obliging as he made a mental note of all that she told him.

*****

The police doctor arrived just before ten o'clock that evening. The main gate into the church had been opened and his carriage was driven up to the front entrance. He sat patiently waiting for the others to arrive. The two lanterns either side of the carriage flickered, their light creating an eerie glow on the headstones nearby. He played with his gloves and took an occasional sip from a flask that he had brought with him. His driver initially had sat up top, but by ten o'clock with the chill air beginning to get into his bones, he had got down and was pacing to and fro. He could hear the gravediggers already at work. Their shovels scraping the hardened top soil. They chatted to each other as they worked, and apparently oblivious to the significance of this event, even joked. Their laughter rang across the stillness.

By ten past ten the chief constable had arrived with the superintendent and another more junior officer. Robert Hall and Father Bolland had been stood dutifully at the main gate since just before ten awaiting their arrival. The chief constable acknowledged the police doctor's presence, did not proffer an apology for their tardiness, but simply led his officers towards the graves. One of the officers had in his hand an object, which the police doctor did not recognise. He assumed from the careful way in which it was being handled that it was of importance. The police doctor continued to sit quietly in his carriage and as he was now beginning to feel weary, allowed himself the luxury of shutting his eyes. He was almost asleep when a rap on his window shook him.

'We're ready for you now, sir,' the young officer announced.

He didn't reply immediately, which prompted the man to say again

'We're ready, sir.'

'Yes. Yes,' he said, clearly agitated.

The cool night air was bracing and he rubbed his hands together for warmth as he followed the officer towards the graves. The chief constable came towards him as he approached.

'They're just exhuming the coffins. Won't be long now. The weapon that we think was used by the killer is here,' and as he spoke he indicated to the object now being held by the superintendent.

'What I would like you to do is determine if this object was involved in the murders. You'll recall that both victims suffered a blow to the back of the head and that the weapon left two precise puncture marks in their skulls.'

'Quite.'

Just before the coffins were raised Father Bolland called for a moments pause, then said a prayer for the souls of John Akehurst and Elizabeth Haines, before he indicated that they could proceed. The light was poor as only a couple of lanterns had been brought to the graveside. The police doctor called for more light and the young officer hurried away with the priest to get a couple of lanterns from the church. By the time they had returned the coffins had been prised open by one of the gravediggers. He had covered his mouth and nose before he did so and it was just as well that he had. The others soon followed suit once they caught the strongly pungent smell, which had risen rapidly into the clear night air.

The police doctor stepped forward to view each body. He was visibly shocked at the way in which they had decomposed so quickly. Their flesh, limp, grey and foul, hung loosely to their bones, much of which were now exposed. He reached first into John Akehurst's coffin and turned his skeleton so that the back of his head was prominent and exposed. He could see the indentations in his skull, which he recalled from his earlier examination. The superintendent handed him the tool. It was heavy and unwieldy to handle and as it twisted in his hands he saw the two sharp metal edges. Reaching down into the coffin he was surprised at how easily he was able to line the edges with the holes in John Akehurst's skull, and so to be absolutely certain he in the object was clearly a direct fit. He stood and looked at the chief constable, nodding to him to indicate his positive diagnosis. He then moved across to Elizabeth Haine's coffin and stood above it looking at her small, withered frame lying there covered in a fine dress. He turned her as he had done with John Akehurst. She had a linen bonnet on her head, which he needed to remove, and he did so gently revealing once more the wound that she had received. He lifted the object and lowered it carefully near her skull. The metal edges fitted perfectly into the wound. Once again he took care to determine the veracity of his finding by placing the edges inside the wound for a second time. Standing up he felt light headed from the odour, the exertion and the rise itself. He turned to face the chief constable and said with conviction:

'This is clearly the object that was used. The fit into each wound is perfect.'

'Thank you,' the chief constable replied. He instructed the superintendent to arrange to have the coffins resealed and placed back into their graves.

At the main gate a group of people had, since their arrivals, gathered. They had watched the event and had kept for the most part a dignified silence. When the police doctor's carriage passed through the gate and turned towards Leatherhead, followed almost immediately by the larger police carriage, they peered at the darkened windows, their expressions vacant.

The priest attended the reburial, watching the gravediggers swiftly and energetically returning the earth to the holes from the tidy piles they had built adjacent to each grave. They worked silently until the job was complete. The two graves now looked neat, the softened soil lying pristine and turned. He thanked them and then watched as they walked across the graveyard towards the tavern. As they reached the main gate they were greeted warmly by the onlookers, who were by now desperate to learn more. Once they had disappeared inside the tavern, the graveyard again lay still. The priest knelt and prayed over the graves before he began to walk to the church.

As he approached the front door, from out of the shadows, stepped Guy Soden. He had stood there, unobserved, watching the exhumation.

'Did it go well?' he asked gauchely.

The cleric didn't respond but just glared and walked passed.

'How did it go?' he asked again.

'Sir, I don't know what you want, but will you please move away.'

'Come on Father. What did they find? I'm keen to know.'

'You might be. It really is none of your business,' he retorted. Closing the church door loudly, he finally found a retreat from the reporter now stood passively outside.

Not finding any success there the reporter made his way casually back to the tavern, where he hoped that even if he couldn't get a story he would at least be able to find a drink.

—〰—

Eight

The club in St James's was situated at the far end of the square nearest Piccadilly. Its entrance was watched over by a well groomed and smartly presented man. He knew all its members and was able to provide them with the courtesy of addressing them correctly as he opened the imposing jet black door to its closed world. Once inside, the warmth of its oak panelled walls and the scent from the log fire that burned in the small hearth in the hall greeted and cheered its members. A large imposing staircase to the left of the hallway was lined with paintings of past presidents of the club, while at the far end of the building on the ground floor lay a charming restaurant, where some of the finest food in London could be eaten.

John Mullay, still bronzed having recently returned from the Caribbean, sat in a dark brown leather chair by one of the large bay windows. It offered a pleasant view across the club's cloistered garden. He gazed for a while to watch a thrush wrestle with a worm on one of the beds, now adorned with early summer flowers. Eventually he got back to reading a copy of The Times, one of several copies left each day in that room for the pleasure and convenience of the members. His eye caught an article near the bottom of the second page.

'Murders near Leatherhead' the headline rang. 'Your correspondent reports from Bookham, a small village near Leatherhead where the bodies of John Akehurst, lawyer, and his housekeeper Elizabeth Haines, cruelly murdered last October, have been exhumed by the police. Your correspondent understands that the murder weapon has been discovered and that police exhumed the deceased in order to determine precisely that this was the weapon used to kill them. It is understood that Will Page, a cobbler, who lives in the village has been apprehended and has now been charged with the murders. He will be committed to trial at Guildford next month.'

Slightly shocked, he had started to read the passage again when he saw Sir Roland crossing the room to greet him. Placing the newspaper on the occasional table at his side, he rose and welcomed his friend warmly. They exchanged pleasantries for a while, ordered and drank a glass of whisky each, before their attention turned as it always did to business. In a hushed voice he described his visit to the Caribbean and his immense disappointment in finding that the plantation was now only just surviving. Without wanting to sound too pessimistic he ventured confidentially to his friend that unless something substantial could be found to make it profitable again, he very shortly might well be financially embarrassed. The problem as he saw it was that since the end of his use of slave labour on the plantation, in which he had also personally been involved as one of the main agents for the other plantations in the region, productivity had fallen dramatically. More importantly having to pay wages, which had risen each year now for the past twenty years, was making the whole venture unviable. As most of his capital was tied up in the plantation, and as he also had significant loans outstanding, due in only two years for repayment, he needed to find the way ahead very soon.

Sir Roland listened attentively, occasionally stopping to ask him a question for clarification, before encouraging him to continue. He didn't proffer a solution immediately, but simply consoled his friend that everything was solvable given a little time and thought. He ordered another drink for them both, which they drank slowly, as they moved to another topic and talked for a while about a mutual friend of theirs, who unfortunately had been taken seriously ill earlier that month.

'Well I don't think we're going to sort it here and now, my friend,' Sir Roland said some time later. 'Let me think about it some more, and we'll talk again when you're next in town. When do you think that'll be?'

They set a date, collected their top coats, and took a short walk up the street, across Piccadilly, towards Shepherds Market. They enjoyed each others company, and one of the mutual pleasures that they discovered and liked to share whenever they were together in town was a visit to two ladies who lodged in that area. Their rooms were on the third floor overlooking the busy thoroughfare below.

The tall, elegant and well dressed lady, who greeted them each with a kiss, ushered them into the suite. Her fine perfume filled the room. Alone at first, her companion, who could be heard moving in the adjoining room, soon joined them. She was darker, had high cheekbones and beautiful smouldering brown eyes. The visitors didn't want to appear too eager, but the girls could sense their anticipation, and so each escorted their visitor to separate rooms, which were located at either end of the suite.

John Mullay had known the girl for about two years and had enjoyed her company many times previously. He enjoyed being with her and she was grateful that he was, compared with most of her other clients, courteous and gentle. Now tired and relaxed, he fell asleep beside her. She lay there quietly listening to his breathing and the sound of the pedestrians passing below them as he snoozed. When she considered it was time that he left she shook him softly. He dressed as she watched with practiced attentiveness, before he bade her goodbye and rejoined his companion, who by then was patiently waiting for him in the lounge.

Their afternoon complete the two men said their goodbyes, Sir Roland retreating to his home in nearby Curzon Street, while John Mullay rejoined the bustle that was Piccadilly.

—⟋⟍—

NINE

They came at six in the morning. Without much ceremony he was picked up by two men from the hard floor where he was sleeping and taken, dragged really, at pace out of the cell, up the stairs and through a door at the back of Union Hall. The air in the yard was cold. He didn't have time to see take stock of much before they tossed him into the back of the wagon that was parked close by. He wasn't alone. At the far end of the wagon was an emaciated man, unshaven, clothes thin and torn. He was propped against a filled sack, which lay there. He looked up with a cursory glance and then began to shiver as he waited for the door of the wagon to be locked. They manacled him to the side of the wagon. It cut tight into his left wrist and he winced. The guard smiled as he noted that, did nothing to ease the pain, simply rising and turning to exit the wagon when he had completed the job. The door was slammed shut and the bolts were moved across and held fast. The wagon was now almost totally dark inside, except for a small slither of light, which came from a spy hole at the front behind the driver's seat.

Will sat motionless for several minutes, listening to the men speaking outside and recovering from the trauma, before he righted himself and made himself as comfortable as he could. The two of them waited there in the dark for at least another half hour, while the men each took turns to go inside and eat a breakfast in Union Hall. Finally he could sense that they were preparing to move off and shortly he heard one of the men give the horses a command, and their hooves then began to grind as the wagon moved forward.

Will knew the lanes well and he could tell from the rises and falls that they were heading off to Dorking before they then turned west towards Westcott. The climb up towards Newlands was made at a gentle pace the horses having to strain, and so when they reached the top of the hill the men let them rest for a while. They didn't talk to each other much, only making the occasional remark to one another, which invariably had them both laughing loudly. And they didn't seem to be overly bothered about their charges either, although at one point Will did sense that the light had been blocked, which he assumed was when one of the men had viewed them through the spy hole.

His back was beginning to ache now, and that wasn't helped by the descent that they made into Guildford. As the wagon dropped towards the river there, it passed over the cobblestones in the main street, shaking everything vigorously. Will flinched and tried to reposition himself to make himself more comfortable, but as hard as he tried it made little difference. His discomfort was heightened yet again as the wagon took a sharp turn and then came to a juddering halt. He could hear as the bolts to the door were loosened and opened revealing that they were now inside a courtyard, which was surrounded by a high stone wall. One of the men jumped in and unfastened the man lying at the front. He tried to get to his feet, but before he could do so he was dragged to the door and dumped onto the ground. The guard then approached Will, unlocked him, and indicated with a flick of his hand for him to get out. As he fell from the wagon his ankles and feet hurt as he started to get some feeling back into them. A man, who had been stood at the back of the wagon watching them, stepped forward. He had a heavy wooden truncheon in his right hand. He shoved it into the back of the first prisoner to get him to move forward and then did the same to Will. Instinctively Will turned as if to react, but he made no further move as he stared into the eyes of the man. He was startled by the aggression and hatred there.

They were ushered through a metal door, which was locked behind them, and then through a second door. They were now stood in a room with a high ceiling. In the corner was a desk, behind which an imposing guard sat. He looked up as they entered.

'Strip,' he commanded.

They both stayed motionless not really understanding what was being ordered. The truncheon was wielded against the back of their knees.

'He said strip; move,' the guard shouted.

They took off their clothes. Will made to fold his clothes neatly, but realised the absurdity of this as he was doing it and simply dropped them in an untidy heap at his feet. As he did so he glanced at the other prisoner, who by now was shaking with cold and fear. Stripped he looked even more puny than he had seemed when Will had first seen him slumped in the wagon.

The guard seated at the desk eyed them before he picked up a stamp and left its mark on the two documents, which he had in front of him. With a turn of his head he indicated to the guard stood behind them to move them on, and a shove in the ribs signalled to Will that he was to cross the room and exit by the open door ahead of them. As they walked, conscious of their nakedness, they passed large cells framed with heavy metal bars, inside each of which sat or stood about twenty prisoners. They jeered as the two new arrivals passed by. Will tried not to be intimidated by them, but that was becoming increasingly difficult and he could feel his confidence beginning to ebb away fast. Fortunately it wasn't long before the two of them were in the comparative sanctuary of a small cell at the far end of the block. They stood there together, naked, in a dark windowless room devoid of any furniture. Will turned to the other man, didn't say a word to him, and then settled himself against the far wall. He began to shiver.

He wasn't sure what time it was, but suspected it was late evening as the murmur that had resounded in the corridor outside their cell since they first arrived had now almost stopped. He could hear an occasional shout, followed typically by an obscene reply; and booted footsteps, which he assumed were guards passing the cell door. Otherwise there was silence. He tried to make himself comfortable. He curled himself into a ball to try and keep warm. It didn't help and he endured a horrible few hours before being wakened from a fitful slumber when the cell door was beaten. The sound echoed for several minutes, shocking him into consciousness rapidly. His cellmate, quiet for ages, moaned to himself somewhere in the dark.

'You alright?'

There was no reply.

'You alright over there?'

Still there came no reply.

'Perhaps the guy's in a worse state than I am,' Will thought to himself.

A bolt was shunted across and the door was thrown open. His eyes were unaccustomed to the light and the man standing in the doorway was silhouetted anyway, so it was difficult to determine what he looked like. The voice informed him. Dark, deep and commanding it instructed them to stand up. Shakily they both did so and as he stood Will took the opportunity to glance at his cell companion. He looked really sick. It took him an inordinate amount of time to get to his feet, and when eventually he did, he stood there wobbling from side to side as if he were about to faint.

'You, out,' the man commanded, pointing to Will.

He stepped forward and shuffled through the door into the corridor. Once again he became aware of his nakedness. This time he cared less about it.

He was pushed up the corridor, taken through a heavily metalled door, and then down a flight of steps that twisted sharply as they dropped. Missing his footing twice he realised that these steps were slimy and damp and were probably not used very frequently. At the bottom of the steps he found himself in a dark stone walled cellar, with a skylight high up on one of the walls. The floor was stone too; cold and dank. The man following him down the steps was joined by a second guard. They shoved Will across the room, where he was confronted with a cage built into the far wall. One of the guards opened its door, which creaked loudly as he did so, and then the other guard instructed him to step inside. He didn't understand what they wanted him to do straight away and so he hesitated. He wished he hadn't done that. A blow struck him on the back of the neck. He stumbled forward and as he did so one of the guards shoved him inside. The cage door was slammed shut and locked. The guards jeered at him and then made their way back up the stairway. At the top they slammed the door and he could hear the bolts being moved across. The room was now silent again. He stood in the cage, his back hard against the wet wall, his knees and elbows touching the cage's cold metal bars. He could barely stand erect. He couldn't turn.

'God,' he thought to himself.

He hadn't at first been aware that anyone else was with him there, but as his eyes became accustomed to the dim light he could see on the other side of the room two shadowy figures. They were sat together on a stone bench that was built into the wall opposite. They didn't say anything, but he could hear them cackling quietly, in what he thought was an inane manner. He thought it best not to say anything, preferring to be careful until he could assess who they were.

After about five minutes, during which time the two of them continued to carry on some kind of strange conversation based on warped phonetics, one of the figures got off the bench and shuffled across the room. He stood in front of Will and eyed him up and down carefully. He put his hand through the bars and felt him. Will reacted instantly, pushing away from him, but there was nowhere to go. Will spat at him, which was about the only thing that he could do. Even that wasn't particularly effective. He realised then that his mouth was dry and felt awful. The man laughed, and then urinated on him, before going back to his seat.

High above their heads a grill opened and a shaft of white light shone down into the cellar. It cast light on the two men and for the first time Will saw them clearly. Both were small and wiry, aged about forty, and each was dressed in trousers and a tunic. He could see that they were both extremely filthy. One of the men had sores on his face, which were reddened and looked painful. The other had a withered hand. When they saw the light above them they sprang to their feet and stood beneath the hole high above their heads. Seconds later a pot was lowered on a rope. As it reached the ground they took it off the hook, on which it had hung, and replaced it with a similar pot that lay on the ground. It was hauled back to the ceiling and disappeared through the hole, which once again was closed.

The two men scurried back to their bench, and he could hear them as they slurped and chewed. He could smell the food, and not having eaten for at least twenty four hours, he soon realised then that he was ravenously hungry.

'Anything for me?' he spoke for the first time.

They ignored him to start with and then one of them to Will's great surprise spoke.

'Wait, you.'

He did what was being suggested in the hope, if only a vain one perhaps, that his behaviour would reap a reward. He wasn't to be disappointed. The second man some five minutes later too shuffled across the room and pushed the pot through the bars into his hands.

'Thank you,' he said as he accepted it.

The man grunted and went back to his seat.

Will put his hand inside the pot and could feel a warm, slightly congealed porridge. He took a handful and ate. It wasn't too bad. He ate it all, scraping his fingers around the bottom of the pot to get the last bits from the edges.

When he had finished the man, who had given him the pot, came across again and took it from him, returning it to the floor in the centre of the room.

'Good?' he said to Will's surprise.

'Very. Thanks.'

Nothing was said for several hours after that. The men settled themselves, and as they snoozed on the bench opposite him, Will tried to make himself comfortable, without success.

The daylight ebbed away and as night fell it became increasingly cold. In the darkness he could hear the two men scuttling around, and then they too finally settled again. His discomfort was now becoming severe. He realised that his mental strength was being tested sorely. He could feel his confidence draining. His father had always told him as a boy that he was weak, and those thoughts and insecurities now started to flood once again into his mind. He had always tried to be brave for his father, but whatever he did never seemed quite enough. His thoughts began to wander back into his tormented childhood, and the incessant pressure that he had felt then to live up to his father's expectations of him. His first memory was a rickety bridge that they had come to when his father took him out hunting when he was about six years old. Below the bridge was a fast flowing stream, icy cold and rocky, and beyond it the woods, where they hoped to trap rabbits. His father let him go in front. The first few steps were difficult. As he moved the bridge began to sway. The more he tried to ignore it the worse it seemed to get, until he felt that he was about to be turned over and tossed into the white water below. He heard in his head even now as he stood painfully in this cellar the scream that he gave then. Again he felt the tears of despair that had then run down his face. His father shouted some expletive ridden abuse at him, and soon realising that they were going to get nowhere, he moved onto the bridge collecting his son as he strode across it. He dumped Will unceremoniously down on the other bank, still screaming abuse at him. The memory was raw. He hadn't until now appreciated just how raw. The memories and hurt began to flow. He recalled the following summer going hunting once more with his father and their terrier Chalky. Keen to make amends and to prove to his father that he was brave, he followed the dog down into the opening of a large burrow. Head down he thrust his body forward. Then he felt his shoulders tight against the side walls. His breathing shortened and very soon he was gasping like an asthmatic for air. Scrambling at the sides in a vain attempt to move himself back he could feel the skin on his hands and knees scratched and bleed. Convulsed with fear, he cried for his father to pull him out. In the dark he felt something move in front of his face. Panic, until the warmth of a dog's tongue on his face gave him some temporary reassurance and comfort. Then the firm, tight grip of a father's hands around his ankles and the painful yank back to the surface. He lay there on his back like a savaged animal, his chest rising and falling, as above him all he could hear were bitter words of recrimination. His father never let him forget the incident, recounting it again and again to his friends until Will was well into his teens. They all found the whole thing hilarious. That was the last time that the two of them had gone hunting.

The thoughts flowed through his mind. His body ached. Then in the dark he began to sob, at first quietly to himself, and then out loud. Across the cellar all he could hear was the mocking sound of two men imitating him.

Daylight came again soon enough. As he stood fixed in his cage, his legs now completely dead, his body ice cold, he could see in the dullness the two men huddled together across the room. It was as if they hadn't a care in the world. Then they were all three roused by the sound of the cellar door being unbolted, and heavy booted footsteps echoed in the chamber as two men carefully descended the steep staircase. One of the men carried a lantern. For the first time Will could see clearly the dungeon, its walls heavy with green slime and the floor littered with filth.

The second man unbolted his cage and pulled him forward. His legs didn't respond. Paralysed. He found himself face down on the floor. He felt a kick in his ribs, and then one of the men heaved him to his feet. The two of them dragged him across the room to the bottom of the stairs.

'Up,' demanded the man with the lantern.

He didn't respond and he felt one of them kick him in the thigh.

'Up.'

Painful step by painful step he ascended, using his hands to help him navigate and climb, until he reached the doorway high above. The warmth and freshness of the air was a welcome thing. No sooner had he had that thought, when he was once again picked up roughly by the two men. They dragged him head down along the corridor and deposited him, unceremoniously, at the feet of a man stood in the middle of a room, empty, except for one chair and a small table.

'Sit.'

Will shuffled to his knees, reached for the chair, using it as a prop to help him get to his feet.

'Sit.'

He sat, once again suddenly aware of his nakedness, as he viewed the man for the first time. He was well dressed, ruddy faced and had penetrating blue eyes. He stared at Will unblinkingly for several seconds, before he moved around to the back of the chair.

'Get him a blanket.'

He heard one of the men scuttle off and return a few seconds later.

'Here,' the man behind him said, as he gently lay the blanket across Will's shoulders.

He moved in front again and stared into Will's eyes. It unsettled him. The uncertainty was beginning to scare him.

'Well, why don't you tell me how you did it?'

There was a pause as Will tried to get his head around that question.

'Did what?' he responded meekly, not wanting to antagonise the man.

'Why don't you tell me how you did it?' the man repeated, coldly.

Will looked up at him. A vague expression now on his sallow, drawn face.

The silence penetrated the room.

'Well let me tell you, William Page,' he said maliciously, 'you're a greedy little man with no thought for what you do or who you hurt. You're only interested in what you can get for no real effort.' He paused. 'And so you heard about the money that was said to be kept by John Akehurst and you thought you'd have some of it. Easy really. An old man. An old woman. Not too demanding even for a shit like you.'

Will looked at him with the same vacant expression.

'And so in you went, armed with a club from your bag of tools. Didn't he tell you where he kept the money then? Perhaps he was tougher than you thought he would be?' He paused and then added, 'so you bashed his head in and then beat the old lady too.'

He didn't say anything else and seemed to be waiting for Will to react. He didn't.

'I'll tell you straight young man. You're going to hang for this. Believe me you're going to hang for this.'

Will could feel his chest tighten and once again his breathing shorten. His face went puce.

'I don't know what you mean. I had nothing to do with those murders,' he squeaked, his mouth dry, his pulse racing.

'Oh! Really?' the man replied in an instant. Dismissively. 'We have the weapon. Found in your possession. We have the watch. Taken off John Akehurst Sold by you in Dorking'. He paused. 'So don't give me that bullshit' he shouted, his face now bright red. His expression snarling. Aggressive.

'Look here, boy. Unless you give me a written confession today I'll have you back in that hell hole we've just dragged you from. And you'll rot in there until you do. Understand?'

Will stared at him, his expression still vacant. Fearful.

'I said do you understand?' he screamed.

'Yes,' Will said eventually, managing to get the words out from his head that was now swimming.

'Right.' He paused and walked slowly round the room. As he came around the back of Will's chair he ran his fingers across his shoulders. Will couldn't help himself shudder.

'Right,' he said again. Now stood in front of Will, glaring, but calmer. 'So let one of my colleagues go and get paper and pen and we'll sort this out.' He smiled. His eyes remained cold and fixed.

Will heard one of the men leave the room. When he returned he placed paper and a pen on the table and drew the table closer to Will.

'Right,' the man said again. 'Can you write?' he asked.

Will nodded.

'Good.' He paused. 'Good,' he repeated.

'Why don't you start by writing this? My name is Will Page. I confess to murdering John Akehurst and Elizabeth Haines at Bookham on 13 October 1826.'

Will sat there. Pen in hand. He went to write, and then stopped.

'I had nothing to do with it, sir,' he pleaded.

'Take him back,' the man barked.

In an instant Will was bundled up by the two men, who had stood behind him. They dragged him from the room. The door to the cellar was unbolted and they tossed him down the stairs. He lay at the bottom, bruised and concussed. They made their descent and picked him up, hauled him across the room, and threw him once again into the cage. Pain shot up his left side. He screamed. They bolted the cage, spat at him and left without a word. With the door slammed and bolted, the chamber was again virtually pitch dark. He heard someone move across the room and felt a hand touch him. It seemed this time to be comforting him.

'There's no use. You might as well tell them what they want. They've got you.'

Then shuffling he moved away. Will heard him settle on the bench opposite. All he could hear as he stood there, compressed in the cage, were whispers as the two men huddled together.

Later that day the skylight opened and a pot of food was lowered. The two men dropped from their perch and scrambled hastily across to collect it and to hook the empty pot. Will watched as the empty pot ascended slowly, its movement jerky, and then it disappeared through the gap above. The skylight shut. The two of them sat in the middle eating voraciously. Will didn't say anything hoping that they would bring him something as they had done before. This time they simply ate the lot, placed the pot for collection, and then hurried back to their bench like two wild animals, who would now spend the rest of the day preening themselves before a contented sleep.

' What about me?' he shouted at them.

He could hear one of them drop off the bench and slide across the room. He now felt his stinking breath near his face as the man clambered onto the frame of the cage and stood imposingly looking down onto him.

'You get to eat when we say so boy,' he snorted, 'and not before then. Just tell the nice man what you did and you can have everything you want. Understand?'

He didn't reply but listened as the man left him and returned to the bench. He could hear the two of them whispering to each other, chortling like two inane beings. He realised now that they were there to intimidate him and were probably earning their food that way. The full realisation of his incarceration was beginning to weigh even more heavily and once more he felt confidence ebbing from him. There wasn't much of it left he thought.

Time passed very, very slowly, interrupted by nothing except continual pain, which intensified hour by hour. His ribs had begun to throb that morning and they now felt viciously hot. Touching his right side he could feel the swelling there. And where he had fallen on the side of his face he could smell the blood, now dry and congealed on his cheek. Emotions began to run. He found himself shaking violently in anger and utter despair, until he could not contain himself any longer. He broke down sobbing and weeping without control. As if aware of his condition, at that point the door above was unbolted and two men came down. One, carrying a lantern, placed it close to his face so that he reeled back in fear that he was going to burn him. The man peered at him and as he did so Will could see through the flame part of the man's face. He was pock marked and his skin was tanned and leathery.

'Ready to tell us all now?' he snarled.

No reply.

'Answer me.'

'Yes,' Will responded, exhaustedly, a few seconds later.

'Good. Then let's get you out of this filth hole, and take you to see the chief. Once you've done that you can get cleaned up and eat.'

Will mumbled something to acknowledge the man as they unlocked the cage and pulled him from it. They were now seemingly more gentle with him, supporting him as he made his way up the steps towards the light above. The second man stayed for a while at the bottom of the steps, where he placed a pot of food, which was pounced on by the two men, who had sat watching motionless.

Entering the room where he had been before he again saw the chair and table, on which was still the paper and pen ready for him to write. They sat him down and as he settled someone from behind placed the blanket across his shoulders. He turned to see who it was and saw the face of a young man, probably about the same age as him. He looked at him and the boy responded with a smile. That simple act touched Will and suddenly he found that he was convulsed, sobbing uncontrollably, his head bowed. The door opened and he recognised the boots of the interrogator as he made his way to the other side of the desk. He stood there. Will began to raise his head to see him, and again noticed the piercing blue eyes. They were now slightly kinder, he thought to himself.

'Well,' he paused, 'are you going to be sensible and tell us everything?' he asked, almost rhetorically.

Will looked at him, his expression clearly showing the deep emotions that he was feeling.

The man gazed back and then leant forward, straightened the paper and pen, and pushed it across the table so that it sat directly in front of Will.

'Write,' he said, the pitch of his voice making this sound more a request than an instruction.

Will sat motionless for a few more seconds and then he drew the blanket tightly around himself, scraped the chair towards the table, and picked up the pen.

'My name is Will Page. I confess to murdering John Akehurst and Elizabeth Haines at Bookham on 13 October 1826.'

Will looked up at the man as he said the words. Hearing those words again seemed slight surreal and Will gave him a whimsical smile. He didn't respond other than to say, 'Write.'

Will wrote the words, and then the man said, 'Sign'.

He dutifully did so and then pushed the paper away from him, almost in relief.

'Good,' was all the man said.

'Clean him up,' he instructed, as he left the room.

They took him to a room in the basement where two inmates, laughing as they did so, threw buckets of cold water over him. Then he was presented by one of the men with a tunic and trousers. The material was coarse and he felt its edges smart his wounds as he placed the tunic over his head and pulled the trousers up to his waist. He was then taken to a cell. On its floor was a mat and a blanket, and in the corner running water coming from a spout in the wall. The water ran away through a hole in the floor. The room was windowless.

Another inmate brought in a pot of food and placed it on the mat and left without saying anything. As he departed the door was slammed shut and bolted. Alone, Will sat himself on the mat. He could feel how tender his limbs were as his body settled on the hard floor. Picking up the pot he brought it to his lips and began to shovel the liquid it contained into his mouth. It was only when he had finished that he tasted how briny and greasy it was. He didn't care. He was just glad to be out of that dungeon. He dropped to the floor, pulling the blanket onto himself and tucked himself into a foetal position. He was soon sound asleep.

—⟋⟍—

TEN

The Judge rose from his bed at around eight thirty. His had been an interrupted night and he was in no mood for small talk or anything banal. As he stood by the tall bay window of his bedroom he could see in the far distance one of his keepers returning from his rounds in the woods that surrounded the property. Below him was the large pond, clear and cool, in which swam the brightly coloured fish that he had collected during the past ten years. His butler had laid out his clothes for that day. Once he had dressed he walked along the minstrels gallery outside his room and wandered down the large winding staircase that today seemed endless, but eventually led him to the expansive open space that was the front hall. New flowers had been arranged in tall, bright vases on the highly polished fine antique table that was at its centre. The smell of freshly cooked foods drifted from the adjoining morning room.

'Good morning, dear,' he greeted his wife as he entered.

Barely acknowledging the presence of the three staff, each stood discreetly to his left, he wandered over to the table where a selection of fresh fruits and cooked items had been laid out carefully on a fine linen tablecloth. He helped himself, and then sat at the head of the table.

Reaching for the newspaper that lay there he started to read, eating bits as he did so, turning the pages in what appeared to be a pronounced and overly dramatic way. Nothing was said between them for at least five minutes, as his wife gently ate her way through a plate of scrambled eggs and salmon.

'Will you be going out today, dear?' she asked, not wishing to sound too prying.

Over the right corner of his newspaper he grunted.

'How about you?' he enquired, not entirely interested in the answer she was about to give for by now he had reached the city page, and was rather more keen to check on how his investments were trading.

'I shall be in all morning and then Dorothy is coming to tea with me at three.'

He didn't respond, and so she finished her mouthful, drank what remained of her tea, and rising said,

'I'll see you at dinner then, dear.'

'Yes, dear,' he said, once again glancing over the top of his newspaper, giving her a quick smile, before he returned to the section on banking stocks.

Once she had left the room the staff cleared her place extremely carefully so as not to disrupt his thoughts, and returned to their positions. The only sound that could be heard was the rhythmic tone of the large grandfather clock at the far end of the room. It chimed on the hour and the half hour. The Judge heard the chimes, recognised that it was the half, and so, aware of his appointments for the day ahead hastily chewed his way through the remnants of the food that now sat cold on his plate, before noisily and rather gracelessly pushing his chair back. Gathering up the newspaper he left the room and as the sound of his well heeled boots echoed in the hall the servants began to clear away the breakfast service for another day.

He settled in his study. His mail, which had been collected from Guildford that morning lay in a small bundle on the left hand side of the desk. He started to open each using an ivory handled paper knife. It had been given to him by a friend about five years previously. He read cursorily each letter putting those that needed an immediate reply to one side so that he might deal with them later. His first appointment that day was John Mullay. He had met the man socially on a number of occasions and had enjoyed hospitality at his home a year or two back. A fairly sumptuous place he recalled.

'Your appointment is here,' the butler announced.

'Show him in.'

The two men greeted each other warmly and then the Judge indicated that they should sit in the comfortable seats in the bay window. John Mullay's personal aide, who accompanied him on most business matters, acknowledged the Judge and then sat to one side of them, his pen and notebook poised. John Mullay remarked on the wonderful gardens laid out in front of them and they then talked for several minutes about it, which they found to be a shared interest.

'Let me come to the point of my visit,' he said, when there was a short lull in the conversation. 'I have an investment in the Caribbean. We grow tobacco and sugar cane there. I was there recently and I am pleased to say that it is flourishing. As you know demand for those two products continues to grow and so I am looking for investment partners. They need to be individuals of note, who want to have the opportunity to have a stake in the enterprise, but who are content to leave the day to day management to others.'

The Judge listened carefully. John Mullay detected that he might just be interested.

'Not wishing to take up more of your time. Is that something in which you might want to invest?' he said, slowly.

There was a pause as the Judge feigned reflection. His mind was already calculating investment returns.

'What type of investment had you in mind?' he enquired, not wanting to sound too keen.

Now more convinced than ever that he would be interested, John Mullay quoted a few numbers that didn't seem to worry the Judge unduly, before he closed by saying:

'Of course, you can help the enterprise in a particular way, and that would give you a much higher return for the same investment.'

'How so?'

'Well it is important that we raise productivity in the coming years in order to get the maximum returns for investors such as yourself,' he said casually, aware that he might be sounding slightly presumptive. 'We can really only do this if we can keep our labour costs down significantly.'

The Judge still looked interested, although now a little mystified. John Mullay thought to himself that it was now or never, and so after a slight pause, continued:

'One of the ways we can do this perhaps is if we can take advantage of transported labour.'

He let the idea hang in the air for a few seconds.

'How so?' the Judge enquired, disingenuously, but fully understanding what was being proposed.

'In the Act that allows transportation the destination is only stated as The Colonies. Up until now this has been primarily to Australia. There is no reason why under the law that transportation cannot be made elsewhere that is within the Empire. The facility in New South Wales has been registered as a penal area, but much of it is actually working farms. In the same way it would be my intention to register my plantation within the colony as a penal area. The real difficulty as you will have surely already noted is that signed authority needs to be given by someone in your position for transportation to take place. The destination and arrangements after that are not actually closely prescribed, providing that that authorisation is submitted to the carrier and to the receiver at the penal area.'

The Judge didn't respond immediately. He simply stood and stared out of the window. John Mullay watched nervously as he did so. He knew from reputation that the Judge was a greedy man and had heard tales told for several years as to how he could be persuaded by money. He just hoped that his proposal was one in which the Judge could see himself being involved.

'Another five percent on the return, payable within one year and for ten years thereafter, and I might be interested.'

John Mullay did not want to appear overly pleased, but he knew that his calculations allowed for a sum like that. He shook his head gently from side to side, rubbed his chin thoughtfully pretending to run the figures through his mind, before replying:

'Increase your investment by five percent and I think that we can be partners.'

The Judge smiled broadly, and then stepped forward to shake hands.

'A drink's called for I think. Jenkins.'

The butler appeared.

'Champagne.'

'Sir.'

ELEVEN

Will's life became routine in the eight weeks leading up to his trial. Each morning started when he was woken by a guard, who banged loudly on his cell door at around six. He had time to clean himself at the water spout before the cell door opened and a full inspection was made by the duty warder. He did the same thing every time he visited, and always ended his inspection by kicking Will's blanket across the floor. Will could never understand what it was that they were inspecting. The room was devoid of any personal items other than that blanket and the clothes that he wore all day, every day. Once the inspection was completed a pot of food would be deposited by an inmate, who followed the duty warder from cell to cell. It was the same inmate each day. Will had never actually spoken to him yet, but they had occasionally exchanged glances. The inmate hadn't responded positively at all when Will had smiled at him during his first week in the cell. In fact he had looked rather horrified and turned his face away as fast as he could, before scuttling off into the corridor. He was a man of around sixty Will estimated, frail and tense, catatonic at all times.

The rest of the day was his own. That's how he played it anyway. The reality was that he was locked in the cell, alone, with nothing whatsoever to distract him. And so he had created a routine for himself. This involved walking up and down; and then round and round; lying on his mat stretching his torso so that he wouldn't completely seize up; and taking mental walks through the countryside, which he so loved. And of course he thought of Mary. He tried not to do that too much as he found it far too painful.

Outside his cell he could hear the muffled sounds of warders passing. He soon learned to estimate the time of day from those sounds, although the room was dark, except for a small slither of light, which sneaked through a tiny grill in his cell door. He learned to tell when it was day or night from those sounds. After a week or two it was listening for changes and differing tones in those sounds that too became an established part of his routine.

He was able to wash himself using the water that flowed constantly from the hole in the wall. But he could feel himself getting more grimy as each week passed. His beard, which had for the first week or two been an irritant to him, ceaselessly itching, had now grown thick and luxuriant.

Not allowed visitors, it was a great surprise to him when he was visited by a lawyer after six weeks. The man was about the same age, but looked considerably younger. Certainly he was more smartly dressed in his deep blue jacket, its shiny buttons setting off a stiff collar and bow. He looked nervous as he entered the cell and was unable to disguise his reaction to the smell. Given a chair to sit on by one of the warders, he chose to sit as close to the door, which remained open during his visit, for ventilation. Meantime a warder paraded menacingly outside throughout the short five minutes he spent with Will.

The purpose of the visit he announced, having settled himself, was to inform Will that a trial date had been set and that he had been assigned as his lawyer. He confirmed the charge that had been made against Will, double murder, and advised, in a matter of fact way, that if found guilty Will would most likely be hanged. The only way that he advised that Will might be able to get a lesser sentence would be if he were to plead guilty and ask for the Court's clemency, in which case he informed that he might instead be transported overseas for life. The evidence he advised was not in Will's favour, and he was sure that the prosecution would win the day.

Will, who had sat cross legged on his mat throughout the monologue stared at him in disbelief, before uttering:

'But I'm innocent.'

The young lawyer seemed to ignore this statement, and went on then to simply repeat the advice that he had just given that a plea of guilty might be received well.

'That's it for now,' he said, cheerfully, as he stood to make his exit. 'I shall see you in Court.'

And with that he was gone. The door was locked speedily behind him.

Will was surprised at how unsettled he was after the visit. Emotionally he had blanked out the reality of his situation. He knowingly had done that, and was actually quite proud of how well that strategy had worked for him. But the visit had brought to the forefront the crisis he was actually facing. He began now to think more and more about his mortality. As he did so his spirits sank deeper. Strangely for the first time since he was put into that cell he realised that he was, and now genuinely felt, alone. Helpless too. With his routine so disrupted by his thoughts most of his time during the following weeks were just spent sat on the floor, where he rocked forward and back, trying to see something other than a very bleak future for himself.

The trial was set for Wednesday that week. On the Tuesday he was taken from his cell and walked to a washroom situated at the far end of the corridor. A warder stood as he was instructed to take off his clothes. As he did so he could smell the stench that was now encrusted in the fibres. He dropped the tunic and trousers at his feet and stepped into one of the tubs that had been filled. The water, lukewarm, was refreshing.

'Get on with it,' the warder commanded.

A bar of soap, hard and caustic, was tied with a string to the side of the tub and he used that to clean himself. His skin stung in places where he found that he had sores, some of which he opened as he scrubbed. He winced.

'Come on,' the warder again instructed.

An inmate crossed the washroom and handed him a towel. It was still moist and Will could tell that it had been used recently by someone else. He realised then that the water in his bath had not been fresh either. In the past he would have been disgusted. Now he found he just did not care. A new tunic and trousers had been placed beside the tub by the inmate. They felt good when Will put them on. Then he was taken further down the corridor and into a room where a man stood beside a tall chair.

'Sit.'

Will perched himself and the man took cutters to his hair. It had grown lank and long and he watched as lumps fell on his chest and to the floor. The barber then frothed his beard and taking a cut throat razor ran it quickly across Will's face, easing away the beard. Nothing was said between them in the five minutes it took.

When he got back to his cell he found that it had been washed down. The floor was still wet and he could see that his mat was soaked. A new, moistened blanket lay on top. 'Washed and brushed, ready for my big day,' he thought to himself. And he began to pace the room. Up. Down. Up. Down. His pacing was interrupted when the door was again opened and unexpectedly a pot of food was slid into the room. He could smell that this was different from the pale food that he was fed normally, and as he ran his fingers through it he could feel that its texture was fuller. He ate it with gusto.

At eight the next morning his cell door was opened and two warders stood outside.

'Out.'

He followed one of them along the corridor until they came to a large grilled gate. On the other side sat a warder. He slid his large frame ponderously off the seat and choosing one of the keys held tightly in his hand, he opened the gate, and nodded to each of the warders as they passed. Having shut and locked the gate, he then walked passed the three of them and opened a solid metal door further down the corridor. It opened out onto a courtyard. Will heard the door slam behind them, but his attention was distracted by the bright sunlight and the vivid blue sky. He was rather taken aback and its beauty stopped him in his tracks for a split second. He felt the warder behind him shove him between the shoulder blades and push him forward to the covered wagon that stood there. There were three short steps up into the back of the wagon and he made these with ease before settling on the bench on the right hand side. One of the warders stepped up too, and before he sat opposite Will, he reached across and clamped one of the irons hanging from the roof tightly onto Will's wrists. When he had done that the second warder shut and locked the door. Will could hear as he climbed up next to the driver, they spoke a few words, and then the wagon moved slowly forward across the courtyard, through a set of large gates and out onto the cobbled streets of Guildford. The climb away from the prison took around ten minutes as Will listened to the familiar sounds outside of a bustling county town.

Once the wagon reached the top of the town it turned right and dropped down a slipway into the basement of the Court House. Unlocked, he was then chained hand to feet and marched into a holding cell at the far end of the building. It was eight thirty in the morning. He sat there for two and a half hours, interrupted only by a very short and rather unsatisfactory conversation with the lawyer he had met earlier, until two warders came to his cell and escorted him up a staircase that led to a landing. The three of them stood there for several minutes. Will went to speak to one of the warders, who looked at him contemptuously and calmly mouthed 'Silence' to him before he could speak.

An usher called from above and the warders pulled him forward and up a short flight of polished steps. He found himself stood with two warders either side of him in a brightly lit, wooden panelled courtroom. At first shocked, he quickly regained his composure, and began to look around. Ahead of him and high above the central body of the Court sat the Judge. Dressed in a red robe and an ill fitting wig that had begun to yellow he still presented a threatening sight. He was preoccupied reading the papers in front of him, which he turned at some noticeable speed. He looked tired and irritable. Below Will were a series of highly polished mahogany desks, at which were seated five or six individuals, whom he took to be lawyers, dressed as they were, formal with wig and black gown. Although he had not recognised immediately his own lawyer, whose head was at first turned away, he did so when the man turned, eventually, looked up at him and nodded. Will smiled back at him, unconvincingly. To his left were seated several individuals, mixed in their appearance, whom he took to be members of the public. He eyed that gallery carefully, hoping to see Mary sat there. He was to be disappointed. That upset was tempered by his huge surprise at noticing Guy Soden sat at the far end of the gallery. He wasn't looking at Will, his head down attentively reading something he had written in a notebook, which he had on his lap. When he did finally look up sensing that the Court was about to be in session, he glanced over to Will, and flicked his right hand off his notebook in acknowledgement.

'Court now in session,' a bailiff sat beneath the Judge spoke. 'Crown versus William Page.'

'Defendant rise.'

'How does the defendant plead?'

Will's head was in turmoil His lawyer had again that morning advised him to plead guilty, but he just could not see how he could do that. Once again he had been assured by his lawyer that the evidence against him was strong enough for him to be convicted, and that consequently a plea of not guilty really would not help his situation at all.

'How does the defendant plead?' the bailiff asked again, his tone showing his irritation. The Judge looked up when he heard the demand for the second time, and he stared at Will impassively.

'Not guilty.'

His lawyer turned and just glared, his face reddening with rage.

The Judge asked the prosecution to set out their case and the prosecutor rose and began his eloquent monologue. His thesis, which he said he would support in due course, was that the defendant had been identified at the scene, that material evidence would show clearly that he was there, that he had motive, and that circumstances surrounding the murders pointed to him having been close to the cottage on the day in question. Piece by piece he displayed for the Judge the evidence, including the principal elements indicating guilt, namely the watch, the victims' wounds caused by the stretcher, and significantly the defendant's own recently signed confession. The Judge showed a particular interest in the stretcher and asked for it to be brought up to his bench, where he turned it over in his hands. As he did so he nodded knowingly.

'A strong case,' he said, as the prosecutor eventually sat down.

'And what have you got to say?' he said gruffly and rather contemptuously to Will's lawyer.

The lawyer rose, and unsteadily opened his defence, which was based entirely on the fact and his assertion that the particular items mentioned had only come into the defendant's possession after the event. The Judge feigned listening. However, from where Will stood he could see that his attention was being given to a sheaf of papers that he had picked up five minutes earlier.

'Thank you,' he said, when it was clear that the defence lawyer's presentation had finally dried up.

Within the hour the Judge began his summing up.

'These are indeed heinous crimes. The victims were elderly and respected members of their community. Unblemished characters. The motive was, in all probability, financial. The method, brutal.' His speech progressed steadily for several minutes. And then he stopped, looked down at his papers for an interminably long time, before he raised his head again. Everyone stared at him, their expressions expectant. He had noted that Will was a young man, fit and strong. Capable of hard work for many years to come.

'This is a young man,' he continued. 'He has shown some contrition for his crimes and the Court should recognise that.' He paused a second time, leaving everyone in the Court staring at him, their faces once again pregnant with anticipation.

'The Court sentences William Page to transportation, for life,' he stated swiftly and in a matter of fact way, his eyes cold and averted from those looking up at him.

'Dismissed. Take him away,' he instructed.

In an instant Will was turned and bundled down the steps, marched at pace along the corridor, the cuffs on his hands and feet cutting deeply into his skin, his chains almost tripping him up. They reached the cell and when they had slammed the cell door shut Will just stood there, frozen, as he began to realise, perhaps genuinely for the very first time, that his life as he had known it was effectively now over. He didn't move, his mind and body shocked. Then he began to weep. At first gently; and then finally uncontrollably. He dropped to his knees. Head bowed. His forehead pressed hard against the cold stone floor.

*****

The six of them sat restless and agitated as the wagon trundled through the lanes. It was early morning when they had set off. The interior so dark made it difficult to tell what time it was now. Will estimated that they had been going a couple of hours. In which direction he couldn't be certain, although he did think at one stage that they might be heading towards London. Apart from one inane comment that a bedraggled youngster had made as they were being chained to the benches on which they now sat, not a word had passed anyone's lips. Sitting three either side of the wagon they were able to look at the others. For the most part they kept their heads bowed, staring at the floor, which creaked and twisted, reacting to the topography beneath it. Will caught the occasional glance from a small boy sat directly opposite him. His fair hair and his round pallid face in the half light made him look mildly angelic. He face remained expressionless. His demeanour sorrowful. At one stage he began to wretch and seconds later was sick into his lap. The others cut a stare at him. One at the end of the wagon said something curt, which contained a number of expletives, before they settled again.

The wagon made a short stop and horses were changed. Men could be heard talking outside. They remained locked in, sweating as the temperature inside rose. The journey resumed after about half an hour, at a slightly faster pace.

They came to a halt, suddenly, an hour later. Sitting there waiting to see what was about to happen he could hear the sharp, incessant calling of seagulls. Then the door was unbolted and one by one they were bundled onto a quayside and into an adjacent warehouse. Along the floor of the warehouse, from one end to the other, were laid a series of heavy anchor chains. At the far end of the warehouse he sighted maybe twenty boys and young men sat in a line on the floor. He could see that they were chained, and he soon came to realise that were each attached to a section of an anchor chain. He was taken close to the far end, told to sit by the guard who had led him there, while another man, weather beaten and tattooed, drew a chain towards him, linked it through his manacled feet and fed it back to the anchor chain, where he secured it.

The warehouse door remained open for several minutes as each of them were settled and he could see then at the quayside a ship. From the activity surrounding it he sensed that it was being readied for departure.

They sat there all day, the tedium only interrupted by the issue to each of them of a bowl of chicken stew, a small loaf of bread and a cup of water. Early on they were amused when they first saw one of the prisoners call over a guard and then defecate and urinate into a large metal pot he had brought to the man. As the day progressed and nature called, one by one each of them did the same, all modesty steadily destroyed.

The following morning, still shivering from the cold that had covered them during the long night, they were roused by the arrival of a further three wagons. Their cargo was brought into the warehouse and secured. They waited all day. Then at around six that evening they were, one by one, unshackled and taken to the ship. Will was one of the last to be collected, having watched the others for about an hour. He realised then, as he tried to walk, why they had all looked so incapacitated. The muscles in his legs virtually had seized. By the time he was pushed up the gangplank some hundred yards away he had just about recovered. At the top someone asked his name, and then he was scurried across the deck to a steep stairwell that led to the lower deck. The other prisoners were sat in rows of five or six on one side of the vessel, and with his arrival he began what was to be the front row. His head was pushed downwards and he dropped to the floor. Fixed into the decking before him was a bolt with a chain. This was threaded through the chains on his feet, and then secured. He sat, head bowed. Motionless.

An hour later the ship began to sway steadily, its movement unsettling. The ropes holding it to the quay stretched, their distinctive sound rising as the tide began to turn. Footsteps could be heard moving backwards and forwards above them as the ship was prepared. Through latticed decking just ahead of him Will was able to see that sails were being unfurled. Soon the ship had a new cadence and he sensed that they were now moving away from the dockside, on the tide, towards the open sea. He began to feel nauseous.

—⚬—

TWELVE

'It's looks beautiful. Stand still. I've still got the hem at the back to finish off.'

Mary's mother fussed around her as she stood in the front room of the cottage having her new dress completed. It didn't help that the cat kept brushing up against her and getting in the way.

'Get away. Shoo.'

The cat gave them both a long meaningful gaze, before taking a few leisurely paces across the room, where it settled on a chair.

'The colour's wonderful and suits your complexion really well,' her mother said, as she worked busily at Mary's feet.

'I know. I'm so pleased I chose that colour. To think I nearly went for something in blue!'

'Well you chose very well indeed; and you're going to look quite something.'

'What time did he say he would be here?'

'Oh really Mary. It's your do. You ought to know. I think he said about seven thirty. The dance starts at eight I remember you saying, so that would make sense.'

'Yes, you're right. Seven thirty. Well that gives me about three hours to have a wash and get my hair sorted. What about the hot water?'

'I'll get a large pan on the fire in a minute when I've finished this last bit. Would you like me to do your hair?'

'No thanks, I'll do it myself tonight.'

Mary and her mother had been living in the cottage for two years since Will's trial. The cottage had become vacant a few months after the trial when his parents, humiliated and eventually distressed having been totally shunned in the village, had decided that they would move away. The two of them had since then restored the cottage to something close to its original standard, and had got themselves into a domestic routine, which suited both of them.

'How are you getting on with Annie these days?' her mother asked, referring to one of the girls who worked on the estate with them both.

Mary didn't answer immediately. She wanted to make sure that she said just the right thing otherwise she knew that if she didn't her mother would start interfering again like she did often, and make things difficult.

'Just fine. She's much kinder to me these days. I think that she's got a new friend, so that helps!'

'Good. I'm pleased to hear that, because she was making your life miserable before, wasn't she?'

Mary didn't comment but relied on a quiet grunt she made to acknowledge what had been said, and to indicate, she hoped, that that would be the end of that.

'Nice girl really I suppose,' her mother continued.

Mary didn't respond.

'Have you finished?' she asked, changing the subject.

'Nearly. One more minute and I'll be done.'

As her mother completed the last stitches Mary lent over and stroked the cat. It purred loudly in appreciation.

'Good puss.'

'Right. That's done. Let me look at you.'

Mary did a twirl, enthusiastically.

'You look really beautiful.'

'Thank you,' she said feeling slightly bashful, but pleased and excited.

'Get that dress off and let's get you tidied up.'

'You need to put that water on mother,' she chided.

'I know. I haven't forgotten. One thing at a time.'

She got up, collected the large pan, and made her way outside to the pump in the alley at the back of the cottage. She was back several minutes later, straining as she carried the heavy pan through the cottage.

'Don't just stand there,' she scolded and Mary jumped to one side.

'That should be ready in ten minutes or so. Why don't you go and get your things together. I'll give you a call when its ready.'

Mary made her way upstairs to get the rest of her clothes ready. Below she could hear her mother humming something over and over to herself. She was happy too and that pleased Mary, although she couldn't help but be irritated by the constant repetition of the same few bars.

'Oh please,' she thought to herself, but she resisted making any comment, especially as her mother had really been so helpful making the dress for her.

She started to think about the dance tonight and wondered how she and Guy would get on again. She had been out with him several times in the past year and she really liked his company. He was different from Will. But in a nice way, she thought to herself, and smiled.

Guy was punctual as he always was with her. After charming her mother for a few minutes, he suggested that they set off towards the hall where the dance was being held. As they made the five minutes walk they chatted in a comfortable way about nothing in particular. Mary then felt as relaxed as she had ever been in his company, which pleased her. The hall was almost full when they arrived and the local musicians were already fully into their stride, encouraging everyone to dance. It didn't take the two of them long to take to the floor. Mary caught the eye of several of her friends as they made their way around the room, and she could see from their response that they were pleased for her. She tried not to look too pleased with herself, but found it increasingly difficult to rid herself of the broad smile that had now settled firmly on her face.

'You look like you're enjoying yourself,' he said to her, as they made their way for the fourth time around the room.

'I really am,' she said, slightly breathlessly, 'I really am,' she said quietly again for emphasis.

'Good. So am I,' he said breezily.

The evening soon came to an end, many of those there having to leave promptly to get their lifts back to town, and so Mary and Guy followed their lead and made their way back towards the cottage.

'Let's go and sit over there,' he said pointing to the bench in the churchyard, on which they had sat together years previously.

'Let's.'

He started to collect small stones from the path as they sat together putting the world to rights, and then he suggested they have a competition to see who could hit a target most often.

'Look there's a target. It shouldn't be too difficult to hit that from here,' he said, pointing at a tin watering can that was lying fifteen yards away.

'Me first,' she shouted enthusiastically, and reached down to collect her own handful of stones.

Taking aim she threw the first stone and it winged passed the target and bounced off one of the gravestones. They laughed.

'Right my turn. Nil all.'

He took aim and threw one at high speed towards the target. It pinged as it hit the side of it and the noise reverberated around them for a few short seconds.

'One nil,' he shouted, jumping to his feet and doing a jig in front of her for better effect.

'Huh,' she retorted, as she took aim for the second time.

Again her shot went wide.

'One nil, still. The leader steps up once again. The crowd hushes. And…' he paused, threw the stone and yet again hit the target.

'Two nil.'

'That's enough of that,' she said.

'Go on. One more go. Please. You can have two points if you hit it'

'Alright.'

Her third shot hit a nearby grave stone to the right of them as it sped from her hand out of control, traversed the flowers of an adjacent grave, before landing a direct and loud hit on the watering can.

'Two all,' she whooped, as she imitated his jig.

He stood and grabbed her by the arm, pulling her towards him. He kissed her for the first time, briefly, on the mouth. She stiffened and then unhesitatingly kissed him back.

Nothing was said as they began to stroll, contentedly, hand in hand, home.

*****

Mary and her mother walked each day the two miles to the estate. Their journey was relatively easy following the track to the south of the village and then along the edge of the ridge through the fields that bordered the estate. During the winter months the walk was often unpleasant as the track became waterlogged and heavily muddied from wheel ruts, with the wind briskly cutting itself through them as it crossed the North Downs. Today was very different. The sun had risen just after five thirty and they had left the cottage shortly after six. The leaves and grass still held the dew that had fallen in the night and the glare reflected in their faces as they made their way at a brisk pace away from the village. They didn't talk much generally other than the odd comment to one another. But Eleanor intuitively could tell that Mary was happy. She had woken breezily, which wasn't always the case, and had been humming a tune to herself for at least ten minutes since they had started their journey. She didn't say anything. She sometimes would not get a straight answer anyway, even if she did ask. Today was somehow different. Her curiosity could be contained no longer.

'You seem very cheerful this morning,' she said, as nonchalantly as she was able.

There was no immediate response.

'Did you have a lovely time last night?' she enquired more directly.

Mary flushed, and turned her head to one side, hoping that her mother would not notice.

'Yes. It was very good. The band was excellent.'

'Good. Did Guy enjoy it?'

There was another pause, and then a dismissively stated,

'Yes, he seemed to,' which was followed by silence.

'Good,' Eleanor replied, after what seemed an inordinate amount of time, during which she had hoped Mary would have elaborated. She evidently was not going to do so, Eleanor realised, as she stepped gingerly over a large rather wet cowpat splattered on the track ahead of her.

'Good thing I saw that in time,' she said, and Mary laughed.

The two of them had been working together at the estate for about a year now. Eleanor's job had become increasingly busy there and her suggestion to the head housekeeper that she could do with some help from time to time fortunately had been well received. Mary had begun by helping her occasionally, but the arrangement was now more permanent. Indeed Mary had inherited a good portion of the work that Eleanor had done in the past and this seemed to have been accepted. They worked together well, although Mary often felt that her mother supervised her rather too closely. She had told her so, and that seemed to help their relationship. What was evident to everyone was that Mary was a fine seamstress in her own right. More importantly than that she was known to be a reliable, conscientious and trustworthy person.

'Good morning, ladies. And a fine one it is too.'

'Lovely,' Eleanor responded to the head gardener, as they passed him on their approach to the back of the house. Mary smiled at him and nodded to acknowledge his remark.

The house felt warm as they entered, making their way first to the room where they had the previous day left their pinafores hanging. There were two other young girls in the room when they entered, who were giggling at a joke one of them had just made. They looked up and then carried on with their chatter, paying little attention to the two of them as they dressed for the day.

'If you finish off the curtains, which we started in the bedroom yesterday, I'll start on those in the bedroom next door,' Eleanor said in a matter of fact way.

'Alright. It will probably take me about two hours and then I can join you.'

'That's fine,' her mother replied, as she fastened the house shoes that she had retrieved from her locker. 'If we try and get that all done by the end of the day we can start on the drawing room tomorrow.'

'Yes, we need to do that. Shall I have a word with the head housekeeper to let her know?'

'No, it's alright, I'll have a word with her myself later this morning.'

Eleanor did not want to sound too possessive, but she could not help feeling sometimes that Mary overstepped the mark occasionally. It would be so much easier to manage her if she wasn't my daughter she thought to herself, smiling inwardly as the thought crossed her mind, but then she wouldn't be as happy here as she was working so close to Mary.

'Let's go and get a quick drink, and then we'll start,' she said, as the two of them left the room, where the two girls were even then still busying themselves.

*****

John Mullay had returned the previous week from a visit to his plantation in the Caribbean, and apart from a brief couple of days that he had spent on the estate, he had since then been engaged on business matters in London. He was tired and felt jaded from the travel and the tedium and, as he saw it, the humdrum of meetings with his bankers and agents. As he lay in his large four poster bed his butler drew back the curtains. The light penetrated the room, rather startling him. He raised his head off the pillows, languorously, and stared out of the large picture window opposite.

'Looks like it's a wonderful day,' he said, positively, to the butler.

'Yes sir.'

'Get my riding gear ready. I think I'll have a ride out this morning. Can you tell the stables to have them saddle Sonny.'

'Yes sir.'

Then picking up the tray that he had brought into the room he said:

'Breakfast, sir,' as he placed it across his legs.

He made no comment, simply reaching across the tray to grab a piece of toasted bread, still oozing with warm butter, that lay invitingly on a plate at the far side of the tray. He shoved it in his mouth and as he bit into it some of the butter ran down his chin.

'Sir,' the butler said, as he stepped forward again, handing him a neatly ironed napkin.

'Huh,' he snorted, as he took it, wiped it across his mouth and tossed it casually onto the tray.

'Is there anything else, sir?'

'No, that'll be all for the moment.'

The butler retreated, silently, to get a bath ready for him and to prepare his riding gear.

Leaving the breakfast tray on the bed he made his way into the adjoining wash room where a copper bath tub, now hot and full to the brim, waited for him. He eased himself in gently and lent out for the soap that lay on a side table close by it. Not a man to linger for long once given to action, he hurriedly lathered his body, and then sank down to clear the suds. As he did so the water splashed over the sides and ran across the floor, carrying with it bubbles of creamed soap that burst as they travelled. He rose from the bath, releasing a second spillage across the room as he did so, and then reached to grab a large white towel that the butler had placed on a rack. He dried himself, stepped from the bath and made his way, naked, back into his bedroom. His progress was marked by damp footsteps.

The butler had laid out his riding gear and he dressed.

The riding boots, beautifully toned and reflecting the daylight that streamed into the room, were difficult for him to get on without some help. Knowing this the butler had anticipated his need and entered the room just as he reached for them.

'Let me help you, sir,' he said, as he bent towards him placing his hand on the sole and firmly pushing the right boot upwards. He picked up the left boot and let him feel his way into it before he did the same again.

'Your horse is saddled, whenever you are ready, sir.'

'Good.'

The butler retreated with the tray and as he did so the head housekeeper entered the room.

He looked up, gave her a kind smile as he rose from the chair.

'Good morning,' he said rather formally, 'how are you?'

'Very well, thank you. Did you sleep well?'

'Wonderfully,' he said, touching her right hand lightly with his as he brushed passed her. He felt the excitement that raced between them.

'I'm off for a gallop. I need to get some of the city out of my head. I'll call on you later,' he ended, in a questioning, and for him slightly unconfident way.

'Yes, that'll be nice,' she replied softly, and nodded her head gently. Her eyes creased and smiled at him warmly.

'Right. Until later then,' and he was gone. She stood in the room listening to his steps as he strode away and descended down the stairs onto the tiled floor of the entrance hall. She heard him pass a comment to someone stood there, and then she moved across the room so that she could watch him walk across the gravelled courtyard towards the stables. A maid entered the room and cleared her throat to draw her attention. She turned.

'Good morning, Louise. Can you make up this room and sort out the mess in the washroom,' she said, gathering herself quickly.

'Ma'am.'

'Lovely,' she replied, as she left the room and made her way back to her office.

*****

The stable lad stood holding the reins, his arm being jerked to and fro as the stallion thrust its head backwards and forwards. Sonny stood tall at sixteen hands and was a proud and distinguished looking horse. His coat, which had been carefully brushed in the last half hour, now gleamed as he began to sweat in anticipation of his outing. John Mullay stroked his neck and patted him several times before stepping up and mounting him. His feet fell easily into the stirrups and he let the reins, handed to him by the lad, run steadily through his gloved hands until he felt the right tension. The horse shifted his hindquarters sideways, his feet cutting a path through the gravel, and he wrestled to steady him.

'Steady,' he called as he did so. The animal flicked its head up and down, causing him to stretch and then quickly correct himself.

The stable lad ran to one side, keen to stand away from the horse, but anxious not to look frightened by it. He looked up and could see small beads of sweat forming on John Mullay's forehead. As quickly as it had begun the horse settled and the lad watched as he trotted towards the open fields at the back of the estate. He was impressed by his style in the saddle and wished that he too might be as good one day.

The horse galloped with abandon and delight across the first field, passed through an open gate at the top of it, before being turned left towards the track that ran down towards Effingham. It moved at a steady pace, its feet caressing the ground, which was firm under hooves. Its breathing was now rhythmic and steady.

John Mullay felt released as he enjoyed the freedom that he had here and a beamed smile transformed his face from a careworn middle aged man to that of a child. The miles ran under him as the two of them moved across the country. They stopped for a breather after about half an hour and he got down to allow the horse to roam up and down a lush hedgerow grabbing the tastiest grasses beneath it. He watched a herd of cows eating at the other side of the field and then saw one of his tenant farmers approach them through a gate nearby. He waved to him and the farmer responded. He could hear him shout something, but the wind carried the sound away, and he wasn't sure what had been said. The farmer moved through the herd, patting one or two of the cows as he did so. Eventually the farmer made his way back to the gate, and as he shut the gate to leave the field, he gave a departing wave to him.

In the saddle once more he crossed the field opposite with the intention of going towards Fetcham along the North Downs path. They joined the track after about one mile and progressed steadily along it until they came to a river. Stepping into the water the horse shied up for no apparent reason. He held the reins tight, but his right foot had jolted from its stirrup, and he found himself being thrown backwards and sideways from the horse. He felt pain shoot up through his left elbow as he dropped heavily into the water. He lay there. The water, which soaked him to the skin, was icy cold. His shoulder was now screeching in agony. He went to raise himself, the pain seared across and down his chest. He stumbled and fell back into the stream. He realised then that he had a dull, thudding pain in his right leg too. He groped his way feeling the bottom of the stream, the stones rough, pushing sharply through his leathered gloves, the skin on his knees being scraped raw as he moved as energetically as he could to reach the bank. He fell on it, gasping for air, his riding tunic, face and gloves now covered with a dark black mud. He lay there motionless for a few seconds, feeling the thudding pain in his chest and left shoulder and the ache in his thigh. He threw up.

He was fortunate as the accident had been witnessed by a fisherman walking down the riverbank, who hastily made his way to his side.

'Easy man, easy,' he said, as he knelt down beside him. He looked at his face and could see that he was extremely uncomfortable.

'Where does it hurt?' he asked.

'Bloody well everywhere,' came the reply, John Mullay attempting to sound upbeat. 'My left shoulder and right thigh,' he offered, more precisely.

'Right. You stay there. I'll make you more comfortable and then I'll be away to get you help.'

Pulling him from under his arms he eased him further up the bank and dragged him out of the water onto a dry patch of grass nearby. Standing up he approached the horse, which was stood ten yards away looking uncertain. He took hold of his reins and tied them to a branch. Reaching over the saddle he untied a rolled blanket that was positioned there and brought it down, placing it under John Mullay's head. The sudden movement made him wince.

'Sorry. Just stay quiet and I'll be back in about half an hour.'

He lay there, soaked and cold, but feeling more comfortable now than he had done before. He closed his eyes for a time, but that seemed to make him focus on the thudding aches, and so he opened them again and tried, with some success, to distract himself by watching the sun dapple through the leaves in the trees that hung above his head. After several minutes he closed his eyes again and fell asleep. He was woken by the sound of a cart and then the footsteps of two men approaching him. He recognised the fisherman and realised that the second man was another of his tenant farmers.

'Sir,' the man said, sounding surprised when he saw him lying there forlornly.

'Hello Mr Black,' he responded weakly. 'Been a bit of a fool here,' he said, again trying to appear in control.

'Let's sort you out.'

The two of them eased him to his feet and gently manhandled him into the cart. They propped him up against one of its sides and then made him more comfortable with the blanket. The tenant farmer took off his jacket and laid it across his legs.

'That should be more comfortable for you,' he said, and then he hitched the horse to the back of the cart, moved up to sit next to the fisherman, who flicked the reins to get his horse to move off. The cart rumbled across the tracks before it settled into the grooves. John Mullay smarted with the pain as it did so. The farmer turned to him, sensing his discomfort.

'Soon have you home,' he said, before he turned back and started to instruct the fisherman on the easiest route home.

They were surprised to see the cart at the front door at first but soon realised that John Mullay was lodged in the back. He looked pale and he could no longer hide the pain that now engulfed him. The butler and a gardener, who at the time was tending to the front beds, helped get him down from the cart. A wheelchair had been discovered in one of the storerooms and they eased him into it.

'Has the doctor been summoned?' the butler asked to nobody in particular.

Nobody responded, and so he instructed the head housekeeper, who was waiting in the entrance hall, to make the necessary arrangements.

'Don't you worry yourself,' the tenant farmer interjected, 'I've got the cart here and if you tell me where to go I'll be away now to fetch the doctor.'

Hearing his suggestion the butler called across to them and said:

'Very good. The doctor is on Effingham Road and is Doctor Prentice. Do you know it?'

The tenant farmer acknowledged that he did and quickly set on his way.

They decided to take him up to his room, where it was thought he would be most comfortable, and so the two of them lifted him in the wheelchair up the flight of stairs.

'Need to lose some weight,' he commented jokingly, seeing how they had strained as they neared the top of the staircase.

'No problem, sir.'

They lifted him onto the bed and the butler began to get the damp clothes off him. He resisted at first, but realised that he was more incapacitated than he had thought and even undressing himself today was not going to be possible. Soon, towelled dry and dressed in pyjamas and a dressing gown, he was propped up in his bed once again. The head housekeeper came into the room and approached his bedside. She clasped his hand for a second, smiled, and then left, fighting back her tears.

The doctor arrived some forty minutes later, clutching a brown leather bag in his left hand. He tried to look calm, but as he approached the bedside John Mullay could see that he was actually slightly flustered.

'Got myself into a bit of a mess today.'

'I can see that. Let me have a look at you. Where does it hurt?'

The examination took a good fifteen minutes before the doctor stood back and summoning all the sternness he could muster, for he knew that John Mullay was an independent minded man, he said:

'Well the good news is that you are going to be alright and should recover soon enough. But you have broken a couple of ribs and your collar bone and you have deep bruising in your upper thigh. I'm going to have to get you into a sling and bandage your trunk, and I'm afraid that you are going to have to take it easy for at least two months while you mend.'

John Mullay looked at him forlornly, taking in the words, and understanding only too clearly the tone of the doctor's message to him. He gave out a grunt of feigned disapproval.

'Thank you, doctor. Just what I needed to hear,' he said, sarcastically.

Once he had dealt with the matter the doctor carefully put his instruments back into his bag, clicked the clasp, and standing with it in his left hand touched him gently on the arm.

'I'll be away now. Stay in bed for a couple of days. Drink lots of fluids and eat properly. I'll come and see you again tomorrow, in the morning'

'Thank you, doctor. I will.'

The head housekeeper returned when they had all gone. She was composed now and had had time to assess the situation. She sat on his bed and held his hand.

'You know you're going to need someone to help you. You're not going to be able to do much for yourself for the next month or two.'

'I know,' he said, squeezing her hand.

'I'll have a think about what we might have to do. Perhaps one of my girls could come and assist you from time to time? What do you think?'

'That seems a sensible enough idea. But let's see how it goes before deciding what to do. You never know it might not be as bad as it feels just now.'

'True. But I still think you'll find a helper useful.'

'Fine. How are you anyway?' he said, changing the mood. 'You look great.'

She smiled at him, leant forward to kiss his forehead, and whispered

'It's going to be a long few weeks. We'll have to find some other way to release your tensions.'

He laughed at her comment, even though it hurt his ribs, which ached so much.

*****

Mary was pleased at first that she had been asked; and then she became concerned what it might mean and wondered if she would actually be able to cope.

Her mother sensed her fear and quickly interrupted the head housekeeper, who was about to continue.

'I'm sure that Mary will love to help him. Won't you dear?'

Mary at first frowned and then gave a weak smile as she confirmed that she would.

'Well, that's settled then. I'll let him know about you and introduce you to him later today. He's asleep at the moment so we shouldn't disturb him just yet. Thank you Mary. Thank you too Eleanor.'

Once she had gone Eleanor turned again to Mary and beamed at her with pride.

'What an honour. Really. And what an opportunity for you.'

'I suppose so,' Mary said weakly, and then more positively, 'it should be interesting if nothing else. I wonder what he's like?'

'They say he's very nice. Charming even. Can be tough though, so you'll need to watch your step. But you'll do fine. You'll see. I'm really proud of you. I really am.'

Later that day the head housekeeper came to find Mary and took her to meet him. Sensing her anxiety as they walked down one of the corridors to his room she said in a quiet voice:

'Don't be worried Mary. He's very kind and he won't bite. He'll like you, no need to worry about that.'

Mary didn't say anything, her nerves beginning to get the better of her.

He looked tired and his face was ashen. He didn't seem to notice as they entered the room. And when they approached the foot of the bed he looked at Mary blankly, which had the effect of unnerving her further.

'This is Mary, sir. She's been with you now for two years. She works with her mother, Eleanor, as a seamstress.'

He eyed her, carefully, up and down.

'Mary. So you think you can help me? I certainly seem to need it. You heard what happened I suppose. Stupid really. Nobody's fault but my own. But there you go.'

Mary hesitated, not quite knowing when to respond. She quickly blurted out, when she thought he had finished,

'Yes sir,' and then for some reason she added, 'I'm sorry that you are hurt sir.'

'That's kind of you to say, Mary. What a gentle person you are. I think we're going to get on just fine. What do you think?'

'Yes sir.'

'Good. When is Mary going to start?'

'I thought tomorrow, sir.'

'Good. I look forward to that. Until tomorrow then.'

'Sir,' Mary said meekly, now beginning to feel a little flushed and her cheeks reddening as she stood there stiffly.

'Right then, Mary. Let's go and get you sorted for the morning shall we. Sir,' the head housekeeper acknowledged him as she led Mary out of the room.

*****

She was so excited when she met Guy.

'You'll never guess what happened to me today. I got to help John Mullay. He had a fall, from his horse out riding, and he's hurt pretty bad. So he needs someone to help in doing things. And they chose me. Pretty good?'

'Pretty good, yes. What do you reckon you'll be doing?'

'Don't know. Getting him drinks. Making sure he gets enough to eat, I suppose.'

'Washing his bum?'

'Don't be silly. Stupid.'

He grabbed her and they kissed.

'Well I think it's great. You'll get to see something different and you won't be fiddling with curtains and cushions all day like you do now.'

'Suppose not. I don't mind that really. Quite like it actually. But it will be nice to see what goes on up there. Wonder if I'll get more money?'

'Didn't you ask?'

'No. Don't be daft.'

'It's not daft. You ought to. Anyway I suppose the experience will be good by itself, and presumably you'll only do it for a short time. What's wrong with him anyway?'

'Fell off his horse and broke his shoulder I think. Anyway he looked like he was in pain when I saw him today. Pretty smart room he's got. Four poster bed, comfortable seating, views over the Downs.'

'Sounds pretty good to me. What's for supper?'

'Don't know. Better get home and see what mother has cooked. Race you to the gate.'

Their relationship was robust and strong and they felt comfortable being together. Guy had been her suitor for some time now, and he was beginning to feel the need for their relationship to become more physical. It wasn't always easy to find the space with Mary being at home with her mother. He shared a room with a friend near West Humble, and so that wasn't an obvious option either. He also wasn't sure whether Mary was interested enough just yet. He needed to summon the courage to move things on a bit. The thoughts crashed through his mind for at least the tenth time that week as they ran towards the gate. He rushed passed her as they reached it and grabbed her as she arrived, wheezing and panting after the chase. He gave her a bear hug and lifted her off the ground.

'Put me down. Put me down,' she demanded.

He placed her feet gently on the ground and gave her kiss on her forehead as he did so.

'What was that for?'

'Oh, I don't know. Perhaps it's because I love you.'

There was an audible silence as he realised what he had blurted out and while she took in what she thought she had heard.

'Do you? Do you really?' she repeated, seeking assurance.

'Yes Mary Ayres, I do.'

She gave him a gentle kiss on the cheek and clasping her arm through his led him towards the cottage. Nothing further was said as they both reflected, somewhat in shock, at what had just happened.

*****

John Mullay had been up since first light. He couldn't sleep. He had twisted and turned, and each time he did so he hurt dreadfully. His butler had dressed him and he now sat, looking and feeling rather sorry for himself, in the large chair by the window. It gave him a wonderful view across the estate. He had always liked the view from there. Now he was beginning to appreciate it even more. He had watched as the gardeners started their work and had seen the stable boy walk Sonny and another horse, which he could not quite recognise, across to the fields in the far distance. They had snaked their way up the track onto the horizon and as he watched he wished that he were out there. His thoughts were interrupted by a single knock on the door. He hardly had heard it.

'Come in,' he responded to it.

Mary carefully opened the door, closed it without making a sound and then ventured towards him. She couldn't see his face but his long legs, stretched out, told her where he was sat.

'Good morning, sir,' she said, slightly less timorously than her previous meeting with him.

'Good morning. Mary?'

'Yes, sir.'

'I suggest that we have some tea first. And then I think I need to be getting on with my papers. They are in the study, down the corridor. We'll go there after we have had something to drink and you have told me something about yourself. Can you call the butler and get him to do that. You do drink tea?'

'Yes, sir.'

She scurried away, not sure what to do about asking the butler to get them tea. Fortunately the head housekeeper was passing and she said that she would have it arranged. Relieved Mary returned and stood to one side, feeling then rather vulnerable.

'Pull up a chair. Over there,' he said, pointing towards a stool at the far end of the room. 'Don't look so worried. You are going to get on just fine.'

Mary couldn't believe how nice he was to her. He seemed to show interest in her and was impressed particularly when she told him about her paintings.

'You must bring me in one or two to show me. I'll be interested to see what you have done. Now then; enough about that. What about your love life?' he said, jauntily. Shocked, she flushed up bright red immediately.

'Ah,' he said, 'we shall leave that one for another day.'

*****

'So he's alright then?'

'Yes, he's fine. We got on really well together. I think he likes me. Wants me to bring in some of my paintings to show him. I think I'll take him these. What do you think?'

'That one's very good,' Guy replied enthusiastically. ' I'd take him that. And possibly that one too,' pointing to a portrait she had done of one of their friends.

'What about this one?'

'Yes I'd take that one too. They're all very good; you know that. Take him those three. I'm sure he'll be impressed. He might even buy one, or give you a commission. Mary Ayres painter to the gentry,' he added, mockingly.

'Silly boy,' she retorted, hitting him across the back of his head, lightly.

'Steady,' and then he grabbed her and wrapped himself tightly around her body. They kissed.

'What was that for?'

'I don't know. Perhaps I love you more than I did yesterday.'

'Huh. What shall we have for tea?'

'I don't know. More importantly, when can I come and see this mansion now that you are such an eminent person there?'

'Don't know. Next week I suppose will be a good time. I think he'll be away in London for a couple of days seeing a specialist. Haven't you been there before?'

'You know I haven't. I'm not important enough to be invited there,' he said, scornfully.

'What are you two arguing about?' her mother asked as she came in from the back of the cottage, where she had been hanging the washing outside to dry.

'We're not arguing. Guy's just being Guy. Do you think it'll be alright for me to take him up to the house next week? He hasn't been there before.'

'I don't know. Won't you be busy looking after him?'

'Well he's away some of the time next week. So I should be free. It should be alright, shouldn't it?'

'I suppose so. Haven't you ever been there Guy?'

'No. All the time I've lived here and never been up there. As I just told Mary I'm not important enough.'

'Don't be silly. Of course you are,' she replied, not noting, or perhaps simply choosing to ignore, his sarcasm.

*****

'What a fantastic view! And what a bed! Wouldn't mind that at all.'

'Pretty good? Come and look at this,' she said, dragging him into the bathroom. 'Nice bath tub isn't it?'

'Nice,' he exclaimed. 'Very nice indeed.'

They went back into the bedroom and stood for a while, in silence, soaking up the view, and then Mary said:

'Come and let me show you his study.'

'That's neat,' he said, as they entered. He went straight over to the leather swivel chair, and swinging around in it he caught his right knee on the fine antique desk.

'Careful. Don't damage anything,' she scolded.

He leant across the desk and leafed through the papers sat there.

'Don't be so nosy Guy.'

He ignored her and then pulled the top left drawer out. It was crammed with papers.

'Not very tidy, your man, is he?' he remarked, casually.

In the middle of the pile he caught sight of a list and carefully marking the spot with another sheet of paper so that he would know where to replace it later, he drew it from the drawer and started to read it. At first he couldn't understand what he was seeing, but then after a little while he realised he was reading a list of people engaged on some project that John Mullay had in the Caribbean. It was headed Gatton Plantation and had columns for names, ages, years and then a section for comments. He scanned up and down the list, which contained around thirty names, and then one caught his eye.

William Page. 25. Life. And in the comments column a cross had been marked in ink against his name.

'Put it back Guy,' Mary said, not paying attention to its contents, more worried about being found rifling through his private correspondence.

He took no notice of her demand but continued to read the document, trying desperately to memorise as much as he could.

'Put it back,' she said again, her voice now a little more desperate. He sensed her worry and carefully replaced the document.

'What was that about?' she asked inquisitively when he had done that.

'Nothing really. Couldn't quite make out what it was. Let's go,' and he got up, took her hand and drew her away.

His mind was racing. He needed to get back and write down what he had memorised.

'I think I'd better be getting back,' he said as casually as he could when they came to the entrance hall.

'Don't you want to see more?' she responded, rather surprised at his sudden loss of interest.

'Another time.'

He gave her a kiss on the cheek and left her standing in the hall bemused, and then made his way at a trot down the long gravelled drive.

—⚏—

Thirteen

He sat in the same spot in which he had sat when he had seen Will Page sent down. The Judge looked a little older and more frail than he had done that day. Perhaps it was the light, he thought, as he settled himself into the back of the hard bench. The court seemed calmer than he remembered. There were certainly less people in the public gallery this time, which he found useful as he could spread himself a little more easily. He watched as one by one the cases progressed. Many were for simple thieving, some for more aggravated theft involving violence, and two were for murder. The first involved a man, who had attacked a young boy when he had insulted him in a park; while the other was a crime of passion concerning a young married couple, where the wife had strayed and had been discovered in their marital bed with her lover. He listened intently all day and took note of the sentencing. His research of the Court's records, which he had completed a week earlier, showed him that this judge had sentenced a high proportion of defendants, all male and comparatively young, to transportation. Some for five years, others for more, and in Will's case, which he had seen in the records, for life. The thought made him sick to even contemplate what that would mean. By the end of the session that day he had noted that five men, all aged under thirty five, had been given varying length sentences involving transportation.

As the light faded he stood at the corner watching the gates into the Court House. The street had earlier been quite busy with traffic and people going about their business. Now things were far quieter. Although he had prepared himself and dressed for a long night he was surprised at how cold he was already feeling as he stood there motionless. He hoped that once he got going again he would warm up. He didn't have to wait long. Just after five o'clock the gates swung open and a wagon, drawn by two horses, pulled out into the street and began its journey down towards the river crossing. He ran to the trap that he had parked a little way down an adjacent side street and pulled out as fast as he could into the main street. Fifty yards ahead he could see the wagon lumbering slowly downhill. It wasn't long before he had closed in on it and could relax. He wasn't sure where it was headed. He assumed to a port. His assumptions were soon confirmed when it crossed the river, reached the track on the Hogs Back high above the town, and then started to head south towards Portsmouth.

It kept up a steady pace for twenty miles or so before it stopped at a stables to allow the horses to be changed. He waited silently in the gloom some fifty yards behind it. Shivering, he ate the meat pie that he had brought with him, while his horse chewed enthusiastically at the side of the track. Some thirty minutes later the wagon restarted its journey, entering the outskirts of Portsmouth just before eleven. It began to rain heavily and he was soon soaked. He hadn't anticipated that, he thought to himself.

At the far end of the town the wagon made its way through a gate into a dockyard and stopped at a guard post just inside the perimeter wall. One of the men seated at the front of the wagon jumped down and showed a tall thin man, who was sheltering under a canopy, some papers. He rustled through them and then handed them back. Nothing seemed to have been said between the two men, and once the man had regained his seat at the front of the wagon, it moved away slowly. Guy watched, and then bracing himself, rode the trap at a gentle pace into the dockyard. He stopped at the guard post and bade a confident 'Good evening' to the tall thin man. He seemed to acknowledge the gesture, but appeared more concerned not to get too wet. He looked at the papers that Guy had given him and looked impressed with the wax seal in the top left hand corner. He handed the papers back and waved him on his way. Guy acknowledged him with a cursory nod of the head, instructed the horse to move on, which it did without hesitation.

He let out a large sigh of relief once he was clear of the guard post. He had guessed right. The guard was illiterate and he could have showed him anything that looked official and the man would have been satisfied.

He could now only just see the tail lanterns of the wagon ahead of him. He followed it for about six hundred yards along a quayside, when it stopped outside a warehouse. Tied at the quayside was a large merchant ship being loaded and readied for sea. He knew the next tide was around four in the morning and so he assumed it would leave then.

Leaving the trap he walked a little nearer to the warehouse and stood in the dark, his back tight against a wall, watching. One by one he saw the men, whom he had seen sentenced earlier that day, brought down from the wagon and walked into the warehouse. Each one of them hobbled, still unfamiliar with the leg irons that had been placed around their ankles. Eventually the warehouse door was slid shut and locked. The two men, who had driven the wagon, exchanged a few words with another man, who went on board the ship once they had departed.

Guy waited for about another hour until he felt it safe to move along the quayside. Passing the warehouse, brightly lit inside, he could spy through gaps in the timber men sitting in rows on the floor. There were at least twenty that he could see. At the far end he caught sight of one of the men, whom he had seen in Court that day. He was sitting upright, his palms together as if he were praying. As Guy watched he could see the man cross himself and then settle.

At around three a gang disembarked from the ship and made their way across the quayside and into the warehouse. Minutes later the first group were led unceremoniously and hobbling towards the ship. They each looked deeply forlorn as they walked unsteadily up the gangplank, disappearing from his sight onto the decking. The discharge from the warehouse took around fifteen minutes and then it was clear from the activity on the quayside, on the deck and in the rigging, that the ship was about to sail. Guy stood motionless. As the dark of night faded to reveal a cloudless sky and a shimmering blue black sea, he was able now to read the ship's name engraved on its stern. Delta.

The long journey home, uneventful, gave him time to reflect on what he had seen. He still was not sure what he had witnessed, but he was now more convinced than ever that he needed to investigate further. He was excited and yet troubled. One thing was certain, he concluded to himself, as he travelled. He knew now that he must not tell Mary about this until he understood it all much better.

The following month he received by way of The Times office in Fleet Street a letter from a friend, who lived on the south coast at Poole. The letter, which had been written several days after he had been in Portsmouth, came as something of a shock to him.

*****

Dear Guy

First my apologies for not having been in touch with you for sometime. You know how it is. But I do hope that this letter finds you well and thriving.

I know you are keen on investigative journalism and thought that you might like to know of an incident that happened here this week. A merchant ship bound for the West Indies had to come into harbour as a member of its crew, a young rating aged about twenty, was suffering severe abdominal pains. Rather than risk his health once the journey had really started the captain had decided to bring him ashore for treatment. He was hospitalised and recovered quickly. The ship unable to delay its passage any longer set sail that evening.

The ship was called Delta. But the strangest thing was that once it had sailed the young rating, when asked what it was carrying, told the hospital orderlies that it was a 'slave ship' and that its cargo were men destined for a plantation in Antigua. His description of conditions on board for those poor souls defies believe. As I say I was shocked. To think that slavery was banned in the West Indies in 1807 and yet here, today, it still carries on.

I am sure that you will find the information useful and something you will want to follow up.

Will look you up when I am next in London. No plans at present, unfortunately.

Your good friend

Joshua

*****

Guy could not believe what he was reading. 'What a strange coincidence.' he thought to himself. His mind started racing. 'What was he to do with this knowledge?' He realised that he needed to have information from the Caribbean itself if he was to be able to expose something as heinous as this and present it to his editor. He started to pen a letter to The Times' correspondent in the West Indies. His request asked the correspondent firstly to investigate the ship, and second to determine the final destination of its cargo. It sounded very presumptive as he reread what he had written. Key was his request that once the correspondent had that information to hand was a third more significant and demanding series of requests. Guy wrote,

'Would you please seek to discover the Gatton Plantation, its ownership and its labour arrangements. And finally the status and fate of a Mr William Page, a friend of mine, who I think is labouring there.'

It must be done he implored himself, as he carefully folded the paper, placing it neatly inside the envelope, which he then addressed, waxed, and stamped with his personal seal. Once he had despatched it he tried, in vain, to forget it all and resume his carefree life.

—◁—

FOURTEEN

John Mullay recovered within six weeks from his accident. In that time he had become very fond of Mary's daily company. He found her uncomplicated, rather naïve ways, endearing, and her humour delightful. She had at first helped ferry him in a wheelchair around the estate. They both enjoyed that, especially once he had regained his strength and enthusiasm for life, after which they would have pretend races around the rose garden that invariably ended in both of them doubled up in a heap, giggling like six year olds. And so, although he had by now fully recovered, he was loath to let her go and instead began to rely on her for the carrying out of daily errands, and more pertinently for companionship. Their relationship, which when alone was one that was relaxed and convivial, to others appeared to retain its formality.

As she entered his room he stood in a long silk dressing gown with his back to her. He appeared not to hear her cross the room.

'Good morning,' she said softly. The tenor of voice made her sound soothing and caring. He turned around, with the gown wide open. Naked.

'Come,' and as he spoke he beckoned her with his fingers.

She hesitated for a second, and then without further thought or care she approached him, and they embraced.

'You wonderful angel,' he said, and kissed her open mouth with real tenderness.

From that day they were very close. While she always felt guilty that she was deceiving Guy, he had been kind to her. Some part of her also felt that he was her master and that he had somehow a degree of right to her. That thought, at first, had unsettled her. In time, however, she rationalised it, and then soon felt relaxed about their exciting, new, physical relationship.

*****

Winter had been hard that year. Heavy snows had fallen in February and had settled for several weeks. Once it had melted the first snowdrops appeared and in early March the daffodils signalled the advent of spring.

'Let's go for a walk. It's too lovely to be inside on a day like this.'

'Yes. You two ought to be outside. The air will do you good,' her mother interjected.

'If we must,' he said sighing, putting down the book that he had only just picked up, and on which he was keen to get started.

'Come on you old crock. You can read that anytime.'

'I'm an old crock, eh?' he said, as he grabbed her around the waist, and then patted her on the bottom.

'Steady. Don't touch what you can't have.'

'Ah. So that's how you want to play it.'

'Come on you two. You're getting under my feet. I've got things to do. Off you go!'

The late afternoon sun danced through the trees as they wandered slowly, arm in arm, up through the village and then along the path towards Effingham. Not much was spoken between them. Mary was happy to have the sun on her face again. He deep in his own thoughts.

They stood at a gate watching some young lambs suckling their mothers, when he finally summoned his courage.

'You know I love you dearly,' he said hesitantly, still afraid to go further, and then almost casually he asked:

'Will you marry me?'

She had only registered his first remark, and was just about to say something to him in response, she had been so was taken aback. The pause unnerved him and he started to shuffle his feet and stare into the distance.

'Will I marry you?'

'Yes. Will you marry me?'

She gave him a wonderful open smile, threw her arms around his neck, and kissed him firmly.

'I take that as a yes,' he said, when eventually she released him.

'Yes, yes, yes!' she exclaimed, excitedly. 'When?'

He hadn't given much thought to that and so blurted out:

'Soon. This summer.'

'Why not? Let's do it. Quick, let's go home and tell mother. She's going to be pleased.'

Returning at a somewhat faster pace, Mary could not now contain herself. Her mind had already started to think about the event.

'Where shall we get married?' 'I know, why don't I ask John if we could use the chapel on the estate? I'm sure that he won't mind if I ask him nicely.'

'Are you sure?'

'Yes, I'm sure he won't mind,' she responded, confidently.

'Alright. Ask him then. You never know.'

'I will. Tomorrow. You'll see. That's the place. It'll be lovely.'

When they arrived back at the cottage Mary rushed in unable to contain herself any longer.

'We're getting married. We're getting married in the summer. Isn't that wonderful?'

Guy now beginning to look rather nervous about it all stood behind watching Eleanor's reaction carefully.

'Oh,' she said surprised. 'That's lovely.' Then reaching for Guy she took his hand, leant forward and give him a kiss on the cheek.

'And you my dear are going to be a beautiful bride. We need to start thinking about your dress. What fabric do you think I should use for it?'

The rest of the day passed quickly as the two of them talked endlessly in the kitchen about fabrics, patterns and dates, while Guy settled himself in a corner of the front room, enjoying the company of the cat and his book.

*****

She was right. He was happy to let them use the chapel and even offered to let them hold a reception for their friends in the dining room. He could not have been more helpful.

'Well I am really pleased for you both.'

He spoke kindly enough, but Mary could not help notice the look of hurt, and also what she thought might be jealousy, in his face and demeanour.

'We'll still be really good friends,' she said, as she rubbed her hand up and down his arm to comfort him.

He continued to look out of the window intently as if he were watching a deer cross the garden, and then he turned and gave her a wistful gaze.

'I do hope so.'

'Oh yes, we can still be really good friends,' she said again just to assure him.

He smiled at her and gave her a peck on the cheek.

'Well we had better be getting on. By the way where are you two planning to live?'

The thought hadn't yet crossed Mary's mind.

'I don't know,' she said feeling rather lame. 'I suppose we'll live at the cottage with mother.'

'You cannot do that. That just will not do.'

She didn't know where to look. His tone had sounded somewhat reprimanding. She could feel the embarrassment beginning to well up inside. Her face flushed and she began to fidget with the sheet of paper that she was holding.

'Oh, I'm sorry. I did not mean that to sound so harsh.' He paused and then:

'I'll tell you what. Why don't you come and live here on the estate? Not here in the house,' he added for clarity and so as not to spook her too much. 'There is a small cottage on the right hand side as you come up the drive. Used to be lived in by one of the tenant farmers. Why don't you live there?'

'Really?'

'Yes. Really. And I'll tell you what, it can be my wedding present to you.'

'You're a kind and generous man.'

'I know,' he said, laughing, as he clasped his arm around her waist.

'Thank you. Thank you so much.' She reached up and ran both her hands through his hair and kissed him on the mouth. 'I'm so grateful.

'Well, that's that, ' he said, trying to make light of it all. 'Back to work.'

—◊—

FIFTEEN

The wedding date was set for the 16th June. As the date closed in on them the level of anxiety in the cottage increased exponentially. There was no real need for that to be the case. Invitations had been sent out and replied to. The menu had been discussed with the chef and the arrangements in the dining room agreed with the butler. Her dress was their concern. They had talked endlessly about it for weeks, and those weeks had now melted away, leaving Eleanor with a massive task to make both Mary's dress and a dress for her single bridesmaid. Every evening and weekend for days was spent frantically measuring and then measuring again only days later. Cutting and sewing. Unstitching and sewing once more. Then just two days before the event everything was complete and the mood changed. Guy, who had watched meekly at each turn, frightened to pass an opinion or comment lest he be severely admonished by one of them, could now no longer contain his feelings.

'Thank heavens! I was beginning to wonder if it was all going to be worth it.'

'Oh, thank you, Guy,' Mary said, chastising him.

'Sorry. That's how I feel. Anyway it's done now, so we can all start to enjoy it.'

'Let's.'

They fell silent again as Eleanor, as she often did, plucked away at something or other.

'It's going to be a wonderful day,' she said, without looking up from her cloth. 'And your idea Mary to ask John Mullay to give you away is inspired. It'll add a really fine touch to everything.'

'It was a pretty good idea, even though I do say it myself,' she said, as she rubbed her clenched fist across her left shoulder in self praise. ' Don't you think so, Guy?'

'Inspired,' he replied, nonchalantly. Mary looked at him carefully, not sure whether he was being sarcastic.

'You do think it is alright, don't you?' she said, looking for his reassurance.

'Of course I do. Yes. I think it was a great idea of yours. And he was really pleased that you had asked him.'

'He surely was.'

'I suppose it's another way of saying thanks to him for his help.'

'You're right. I think it is. Anyway I can't think of anyone else I would have wanted to give me away, other than my father of course.'

'No. He's a great choice. And we're both lucky.'

'Where's your suit, Guy?' Eleanor asked, again, without looking up from the hem she was fixing.

'Neatly tucked away.'

'Has Mary seen it?'

'Of course I have mother. It looks really smart. Doesn't it?'

'I thought so. But then again what doesn't look good on me?' he said, half jokingly. She squished a hand in his general direction, and then leant forward and gave him a kiss on the cheek.

'What's that for?'

'For being you.'

'Right. I'll have to try to be that again.' Their laughter made Eleanor stop for the first time.

'It's going to be wonderful,' she said. 'Just wonderful.'

*****

The service was held in the chapel. It had been decorated beautifully with seasonal flowers matching the bouquet that Mary held in her hand as she walked towards it on his arm.

'Ready?'

'Too late now,' she said, jokingly. 'Yes I'm ready. And thank you once again for being so kind to me.'

'It really is my pleasure,' he said, as he squeezed her hand. 'It really is.'

Entering the chapel they heard the organ strike up a powerful melody and the congregation of around fifty stood, turned, and strained to watch as they walked slowly towards the altar. There Guy stood looking serious and slightly nervous, until Mary came close to him and gave him a loving smile. The service began and, like many other couples had experienced before them, was to their great surprise over before they knew it. They were soon on their way down the aisle, a sea of happy smiling faces beaming at them from every pew.

The wedding breakfast, which was attended by John Mullay and their closest friends, was a beautiful occasion. The food as the chef had promised Mary was presented exquisitely and tasted wonderful. The champagne and wines, selected carefully from his cellar, were quaffed eagerly. As each bottle fell dry the noise in the dining room rose until it was difficult to talk to anyone other than the person sat next to you. The gong did silence them once, rather abruptly, allowing John Mullay to toast the two of them to the cries of 'Mary and Guy.'

By nine, as the sun was beginning to set, they announced their departure and settled into the carriage that had waited for them during the evening at the front door. Two fine black horses, their necks adorned with flowers, stood tall and steady, until the driver, himself resplendent in a red top coat and a black top hat, gave the instruction to move away. With ease the horses picked up and moved swiftly down the drive, the farewells fading into the warm air as they did so.

They looked at each other and burst out laughing.

'What a day! What a great day that was?'

'Certainly was, Mrs Soden.'

He reached across and took her hand. She leant towards him and they kissed as the carriage took them to their new home on the edge of the long drive.

*****

Life on the estate following the wedding was peaceful and domestic. Mary retained her role helping John Mullay, while Guy's career began to develop at a pace. He was now spending several weeks a month in Fleet Street working alongside the editor, which meant that he was often away living in digs near Farringdon. Much of their time on the estate was spent together. They enjoyed simple things like walking around it and off onto the paths that led away from it. They even started to garden and were proud of the vegetables that they ate in the summer from their endeavours. Occasionally he would call on them to see how they were getting along and he would sometimes ask Guy if he would like to join him when he went shooting. Squeamish, and also rather reluctant to spend time on such pastimes, he had always politely declined the offer. A regular visitor to the house was Eleanor. She would call in on her way onto the estate and then Mary and she would walk up to the house together. At least once a week she would spend an evening with them before making her way back home. Mary enjoyed her company, especially now that Guy was away, but she was also happy enough to have time to herself. She could not have been much more content than she now felt.

It was late in the year when a letter addressed to Guy arrived in Fleet Street. He knew immediately that it was from his colleague in the West Indies. Excitedly he opened it and began to read.

*****

Dear Guy

It is some time since I received your letter and so I apologise that it has taken so long for me to reply to you.

My enquiries have not been easy to undertake. Nevertheless, I am able to confirm to you that the Gatton Plantation is a working plantation in Antigua growing large quantities of sugar cane and some tobacco. It is owned by John Mullay. He is not based here in the West Indies, although he does travel here regularly. The plantation has been in existence for many years and in the past relied for its labour on slaves from West Africa. In more recent times some of these slaves, since freed, have continued to work on the plantation as employees, and I understand that some today have jobs supervising the work of others. I was disturbed to discover that recently the plantation has registered itself as a penal colony, which it clearly is not, and that it is being supplied from England with convicts transported here. There are now around five hundred convicts here. They work in the fields, as the West African slaves did in the past. Life for them is hard and brutal.

You were especially interested in William Page. It is a great regret to me that I have to inform you that he was here. Sadly he passed away from dysentery earlier this year. He is buried in a cemetery on the plantation.

You will be shocked by the information I have been able to give you. I am certain that as a colleague you will want to expose this practice. My advice is to be patient and extremely careful.

Your colleague.

Thomas Foster.

*****

Guy reread the letter several times. Each time his heart sank. He thought once again if he should tell Mary. On balance he thought that it would be best if she did not know. It would only upset her. There was no point in doing that he felt. Anyway he needed to investigate everything a little more deeply before he could divulge a story like this, and that would certainly take time. That evening he spent writing notes about what he had discovered and tucked the letter between the pages of his folio for safety and as a marker.

One of the aspects of estate life that Mary enjoyed was going to the chapel on a Sunday morning. The two of them had become regular churchgoers since the wedding. It gave them the chance as well to meet socially others on the estate. John Mullay had noted their attendances and in the summer had invited them to sit alongside him in the front pew. While Mary was thrilled to be there Guy found it less comfortable. He was not a particularly devout churchgoer. The service, which many would have considered to be low church, he still found over elaborate.

He had not yet been confirmed and so sat and watched as Mary, accompanied by John, stepped forward during the service to take Holy Communion. John Mullay always carried with him to the service a black leather bound Holy Bible, which he clutched in his left hand and held to his chest. He would even take it with him as he took communion, until one Sunday, when inadvertently he left it next to Guy. Wanting to pass the time as he sat there patiently waiting their return he picked up the Bible and flicked casually through the pages. He came to a page at the top of which, in John Mullay's hand, was written 13 October 1307, and underneath that were the words Deuteronomy 32:35. Below these headings was a list of dates and names. His eye fell instantly to two on the page. John Akehurst and Elizabeth Haines. Beside their names was written a date. 1826.

He felt the blood rush from his face and a cold sweaty shiver slid across his shoulders and down his back bone. He stared again at the page, and then feeling conscious that others might be watching him, he slowly closed the

Bible and replaced it, precisely, where it had lain. Staring ahead, his eyes vacant, his mind racing, he was brought back by Mary nudging his knee as she returned to her seat.

'What's got into you?' she whispered, once she had settled herself.

'What?'

'You look terrible. Are you sure you're alright?'

John returned and sank to his knees to pray before rising again. He turned to Guy and smiled. Guy felt the skin in his face tighten as he looked into his eyes. Quickly he averted his gaze. He sat uncomfortably for the remainder of the service unable to comprehend anything that was being said, and only regaining his sense of reality when Mary dug him in the arm and stood.

'Come on Guy,' she chided, and then turned to make her way from the pew. He followed, his footsteps leaden, his breathing shallow, his thoughts frenetic.

*****

Guy thought throughout the following three weeks about what he had seen and found it difficult not to stare at the leather bound Holy Bible each time he saw it being carried into the chapel and as it rested so near him during the service. He never had another opportunity to touch it, and certainly not to reopen it to rediscover the page he had read. Eventually, he decided that he could not ignore any longer what he had witnessed, and that he had at least, as a start, to find out more about John Mullay. He hoped that that might help him to understand and make sense of what he had seen. And so the next week when he was once again in London he took the opportunity to visit a friend of his, who worked close to the Strand, and who had an interest in genealogy.

'So you say his name is John Mullay? What do you know about his background?'

'Nothing really. I know that he has a plantation in the West Indies, but I'm not sure when he acquired that. I know that the estate on which he lives has been established for six or seven hundred years. I learnt that much at school, when we studied local history. His house isn't as old as that. That I think was built less than a hundred years ago. Oh, and I do know what his coat of arms looks like. Here, let me draw it.'

Guy grabbed his folio and began to draw it on one of the pages. As he did so he spoke.

'He's got two red crosses. One is in the upper left corner and the other in the bottom right. And then the top right is shaded blue with a gold line diagonally cutting across it. The blue is light blue. A bit like your eyes. The pattern is repeated in the bottom left section. Like this.' He turned the page towards his friend as he finished drawing.

'Can I take that?'

'Sure.'

Guy carefully tore the page from the folio and handed it to his friend, who stared at it for a while before folding it neatly and putting it into his pocket.

'How long are you up this time?'

'Just until Friday. I'll make my way back to Surrey in the afternoon.'

'When are you back after that?'

'Not for a couple of weeks. Does that give you enough time?'

'Might be able to do something this week, although I am busy most of the time. I'll let you know if I do get a move on. Otherwise, why don't we have a drink again when you're next up and I'll let you know what I've been able to find then?'

'Sounds good to me,' although inwardly Guy had hoped to know a little sooner. 'Yes, same place?' he added, trying to appear relaxed about the arrangement.

'Why not? Let me know what date's best for you.'

'Fine. Wednesday's probably best. Another drink?'

'Sure. Thanks.'

*****

'Good morning! How are you both today?'

'Great. Lovely day isn't it?'

The two of them passed through the back entrance to the house, brushing passed one of the chefs, who had greeted them as they did so. They made their way towards the front hall. Guy followed a pace or two behind Mary as she strode confidently up the staircase that led to his quarters.

'Are you sure it's alright for me to be with you?' he asked again, as they got to the landing at the top of the staircase.

'Of course it is. As long as you don't make a mess or break anything.'

'I'll see that I don't,' he said, sarcastically.

The study door was shut and so Mary knocked and waited before entering.

'He must still be in bed. It is only just past eight thirty I suppose.'

Once inside Mary searched for the papers she had left in the room the previous day and needed that morning, when she was due to go into Leatherhead for him.

'I'm sure I left them on the desk,' as she lifted and thumbed her way through a pile that was sat there.

Guy stood by the door feeling at first nervous, and then when Mary had failed to find the papers immediately, slightly agitated.

'I thought you said it would only take a few minutes.'

'It will. They're here somewhere. Unless he's moved them since yesterday.'

Guy sighed in a way that indicated his displeasure at having to wait and then he wandered from the door and began to run his eye across the books that were neatly stacked on the shelf along the far wall. He was surprised at the range of books there. Many indicated John Mullay's interest in farming and rural pleasures, but quite a few were works of fiction by many of the current leading authors. He pulled several off the shelf and flicked through the pages before replacing each with great care. As he replaced the third book he had pulled out he caught site of the black leather bound Holy Bible that he had seen in the chapel. Hesitating at first he resisted reaching up for it. Then impulsively and driven by a need to know more he leant forward, stretching, and gently squeezing the cover between his fingers to grab hold of it, he brought it down into his left hand.

He wasn't sure where previously he had seen the list, and so he turned over the pages as rapidly as he could in the hope that he would find it without too much fuss. At first he couldn't see it but on a second run through the pages he caught sight of writing and catching the pages he went back through them one by one until the list was once again there in front of him. It looked to him essentially as he had remembered it, although he was rather surprised at a second look to realise that the list of names, including John Akehurst and Elizabeth Haines, numbered eight. There was a name and a year listed against each, the last being 1831, the year previous. The name against that date was Matthew Royce. He stared at the name. It seemed familiar, but he couldn't immediately recall how or why. He was lost in his thoughts when the door was pushed open and in its frame stood John Mullay. He had seen Mary, but was rather surprised when he then caught sight of Guy, who had by then turned to see who had entered. He stood there with the Holy Bible, still open at the page on which the list was written, in his hands. He instinctively shut the Holy Bible and made to return it to its position on the shelf.

'Please,' he said sternly, extending his hand to indicate to Guy that he should hand the Holy Bible to him.

Guy stepped towards him and placed it softly into his upturned palm.

'Sorry.'

He didn't reply, but simply stared at him coldly. Guy could sense his aggression and reacted by stepping around him and leaving the study.

'What are you looking for?' he said more gently to Mary, who had now stopped shuffling papers.

'The papers that you wanted me to take to Leatherhead this morning. I'm sure I left them here on the desk,' she said putting her hand down on the desk to indicate the place, where she had expected to retrieve them.

GRIEVOUS LOVE

'Ah, those. I was rereading them last night. They're on the desk in my bedroom. Why don't you go and get them?'

'Right. I knew I had put them there,' she remarked, as she brushed passed him, touching him gently on his arm as she did so. They exchanged the briefest of smiles, before Mary walked down the corridor, where Guy was standing uncomfortably, towards his bedroom.

Returning a minute or two later she stood in the study door and waved a cheery goodbye to him. He was now seated at his desk and looked up to acknowledge her.

'See you later,' he said, and pursing his lips he blew her a kiss. She returned the compliment.

—◊—

Sixteen

The stagecoach steadied and then stopped as it reached Leatherhead. Guy got down, bid the driver a cheery goodnight, and started the walk up towards Bookham. Although tiring, the last fortnight away from Mary and domesticity had given him time to continue to see friends in London, and to work on the article he had been writing since the end of the summer. As he headed up the hill he felt the chill wind bite into his jacket. He started to shiver and so held his gloved hand to his collar to try and keep out the cold. By the time he had reached the top he was feeling warmer, although a good deal more tired. Nights out in the past week were, he thought, beginning to catch up with him. A trap running the other way passed him and the driver waved and shouted something that he didn't catch. He waved back and turned to watch as it dropped down over the brow of the hill.

Rain began to fall, at first just spitting, and then after five minutes more heavily. He hastened his step. His shoes, which he had only cleaned that morning, were soon muddied and he could feel his feet beginning to get wet and cold. He cussed under his breath.

He didn't hear anyone behind him but he did feel the blow that was rained onto the back of his head. Falling heavily to the ground, his face hit the gravelled surface and he felt his right cheek bone crack and thicken instantly. He lay there, sprawled, and then felt someone yank him to his feet and pull him into the undergrowth at the side of the road. He could see the boots of a second man stood by his forehead as he lay there. The man bent down and unceremoniously wrapped a rough material, some kind of sacking, he thought, tightly around his eyes; and then a second piece across his mouth. Both pieces the man tightened and knotted at the back of Guy's head. He could now feel the blood pumping in his temples. His mouth was drying and he felt a continuous sharp pain where one of his teeth had been dislodged. While one of the men then tied his hands behind his back, the other tied his feet together. Lying there, prostrate, he gasped heavily for breath. One of the men put his hands under his armpits and dragged him the ten yards or so towards a wagon that was standing nearby. He threw his upper body onto the floor of the wagon, while the other man finished the job by hauling Guy's feet up and into it. They pushed him forward scraping his face along the floor, splitting open his cheek, which by now had puffed up to the size of an orange. He could feel the liquid drain from the wound, and then it began to hurt beyond belief.

One of the men stayed in the back with him while the other went up front and drove the wagon. They drove for about half an hour until they came to a lane, when they turned, the wagon rocking and rolling as it edged up the sodden rutted track.

'Here?'

'Yes.'

The wagon door was opened and the man, who had sat with his foot pressed into Guy's back, jumped down. He felt them grab his feet and pull him towards them. He dropped off the end and his face hit the muddy track full bore. His nostrils filled with mud and water and he gagged and groped as he gasped for oxygen.

Each man grabbed him by an arm and face downwards he was dragged across a field. They lifted him onto a brick ledge and propped his chest on it, before one of then took hold of his feet and then tumbled him headlong, downwards, into a well. He hit its sides as he fell and the force scalped the back of his head. Seconds later, with his body twisting and spinning, his face banged hard against the wall, crushing his nose, and tearing off his lips.

Looking down they heard him hit the water. In the blackness they didn't see his feet bob to the surface a little later. Laughing they ran back to the wagon and turned it towards home.

That same evening John Mullay stood on deck watching the lights of Portsmouth fade as the ship moved gracefully up the Solent, headed for the Caribbean.

*****

It was extremely hot the following summer. As their cattle huddled tightly under the trees throughout the day for shelter the two farmers dropped their line into the well. They heard the telltale splash and then began to pull the pan up from the depth. By the time they had heaved it to the top they were both sweating profusely.

'God that's heavy.'

'Certainly is. I'm wringing.'

'Stinking more like.'

'Steady, otherwise you might find yourself down there,' and as he gestured towards the bottom of the well he caught sight of the lower half of a leg, its foot still inside a shoe.

'Christ. Peter!'

Peter stopped gazing across the field and turned his attention back to his friend. As he did so he too saw it.

'My god! What's that?'

'Looks like a shoe to me,' the other said as they both heaved the pan over the wall around the well and dropped its contents onto the grass. The water, sour looking and fetid, ran away and disappeared in an instant into the parched earth.

They both stared at the leg and single shoe, uncertain what to do, before Peter had the courage to wrap it into a sheet, which they had in the cart.

'We had better take this to the police house.'

'Suppose so.' Then he added without irony ' I don't know what the cattle are going to drink now. Let's hope it rains.'

The following day constable Hall came to the well with the two men and bravely had himself lowered into the darkness. He knew he was being foolish. As he hung there the rope swung unsteadily as they lowered him, inch by inch. He held the lantern tight and peered into the abyss below him. He began to feel ill. It wasn't only the drop, unsettling and unnerving as it was, but the putrid smell that he was now sucking in through his nostrils. He felt even worse when the light shone across the top of the water, in which he could now clearly see lay a crumpled, decomposing corpse.

'Steady. Steady,' he screamed up the face of the well. 'Two more feet only.'

'Two?'

'Two. Yes, two!'

He could see that the legs of the corpse were bound hand and feet and as he leant to stretch down to lower the lantern further to get a better look he saw that the corpse's face had disappeared, and that the back of the skull had been horribly crushed. He could not contain himself any longer and proceeded to be violently sick, holding as tightly as he could to the rope.

'Up! Up!,' he yelled.

The air at the surface was the best that he had ever tasted in his entire life.

'Well done you,' one of the farmers said, as they both heaved him over the wall and eased him to the ground.

Sweating heavily, he rubbed his sleeve across his forehead, and then began to cry.

'Steady man. It's alright. You're safe now,' Peter said trying to calm him, as he placed a hand on his right shoulder.

'There's a corpse down there alright,' he said some while later. 'I'll need to arrange to have the boys from Union Hall get it out. I don't know how long it's been there but I can assure you the smell at the bottom of that well is something else.'

'Better not water the cattle with it then,' the other said, trying to lighten things, but only ending up sounding unsympathetic.

'Jim! ' Peter scolded.

'Sorry.'

*****

The corpse was brought to Union Hall at the end of the following day and the police doctor arrived that evening to carry out his post mortem examination. He recognised from the state of the body that it had probably been in the water for under a year and it was obvious to him that the man had died from the trauma to his skull as he had fallen. There were no obvious identifying marks although they did have his shoes, clearly a smart pair with a neat buckle, and in his jacket pocket they found a small notebook. Surprisingly some of the text in it was still legible. From the occasional words that could be deciphered it was evident that the man had written about events that he had witnessed and was most probably someone who wrote for a living, possibly a journalist. Nevertheless his identity remained a mystery for several weeks until Guy's mother noticed an article in a newspaper that she had bought earlier that month. There was a description of the shoes beside a short piece about the find, together with a drawing of the buckle. It certainly looked like the pair that she had bought for Guy's birthday only last year. Venturing down to Union Hall her worst fears were soon confirmed.

The burial took place three weeks later at the church on the hill in Reigate where Guy's parents still lived. Mary had been inconsolable for days after she had been informed, as gently as he could, by the constable. She sat next to her mother and Guy's parents as the local priest officiated at the service. Throughout the service her head was bowed while her eyes, which had been puffed and red for days, made her look extremely sad beyond mere words. Her face, gaunt and beginning to look hollowed, was as pale as milk. She coughed, nervously, time and time again.

Behind her was a colleague of Guy's from Fleet Street. He had difficulty holding back the tears too as he sat and listened to the service. He was saddened deeply to see Guy's widow in such distress. As he left the church he made sure to introduce himself to Mary.

'I'm so deeply sorry about everything.'

'Thank you.'

'If there's anything I can do, please do let me know. I was a colleague of Guy's in Fleet Street. He was a good and capable man.'

'Yes.'

'There is something I found only the other day, which belonged to him. You may want to keep it,' and as he spoke he handed her a folio, which was tied shut with a purple bow.

'Oh. Thank you. That is kind of you.' She realised as she looked at him properly for the first time that she didn't know his name.

'Sorry. I didn't catch your name.'

'Michael. Michael Snow.'

'Thank you, Michael. That's very thoughtful of you.'

As she completed the sentence she moved quietly away from him and descended the eight steps that took her onto the road, where a carriage was waiting for her. Staring out of the window, aimlessly, she twiddled with the bow as she was driven back to her house on the estate.

*****

Over the following six months Mary regained her strength and put far behind her the fragile state, into which she had fallen since Guy had disappeared just one year earlier. The first few months after he had not returned home that evening as she had expected were days in which she was constantly tormented, and when she felt full of extreme anguish. Nothing or nobody could settle her or bring her any kind of comfort. As month followed month she settled back into some semblance of a routine. Nevertheless, she found time after time during each hour her mind wandering, questioning, searching for some trace of knowledge about what had become of him. She had just about begun to reconcile herself to his loss when his body was discovered. That as might be expected had once more brought her great distress. To know the nature of her loss was what she had wished. Actually to gain that knowledge was more than she could at first bear. But, as time passed, her mind eased, and she steadily once more became her old self, lively, energetic and positive about life.

Seeing her change and come back to life was a great pleasure for everyone to watch. Her mother, who throughout the past year had tried her level best to bring comfort, was pleased. John Mullay, who for months had tried to encourage her to be more active and join in the social events to which he had taken to inviting her, was especially happy. Their relationship had since her marriage to Guy been essentially platonic. There had been one or two occasions when memories of the past had surfaced and the strength of their desire for each other needed to be satisfied. Now, however, freed from her vows she was able and ready to resume a more permanent liaison with him. He was thrilled, of course, particularly now that his head housekeeper had decided to leave the estate to take up a new appointment with a wealthy family in the neighbouring county of Kent.

They had spent the afternoon alone in his bedroom. She praised him for his attentiveness.

'Well you're a fine wine, and as they say a fine wine needs to be drunk and not kept in a dark cellar.'

'Is that where you think I've been?' In a dark cellar?'

'Yes. A dark cellar. Well you could describe it as that. Life has been really tough for you. But it's going to be so much better now. You'll see. And anyone who stands in the way of that had better watch out.'

'Danger,' she responded, mocking him. ' Do you really think it's going to be good for us?'

He didn't respond immediately. He propped himself up against the imposing headboard of his four poster bed, cast a quick glance at the light fading outside, and then turning towards her his face inches above hers, replied:

'Yes I do. And what's more I would like the rest of your better life to start today. I want you to move in to the main house. To be here, with me. In this bed every night.'

She stared up at him and as she did so a broad smile crossed her pink face.

'Is that a yes then?'

'Might be,' she teased.

'Well. Will you. Will you come and live with me here?'

She raised her head and kissed him. She felt his weight on her again as they embraced.

'Good. That's settled then,' he said. 'I'll have your things brought into the house tomorrow.'

'No. No. Let me sort things out for myself. Besides I need to tell mother. She might not be so pleased. But she does need to be told by me. I'll speak to her in the morning and we can take it from there.'

'Alright. As you wish.'

There was a gentle knock and the butler entered the room, which now was darkening. Not seeing the two of them at first he moved across the room and drew the curtains. John Mullay gave a small cough, which made the butler jump and turn towards the sound.

'Oh, I'm most terribly sorry, sir. I didn't realise you were in the room. I'll come back later.'

'You do that,' he said, curtly.

'Sir,' he replied, discreetly glancing at Mary, who lay there, the Egyptian linen sheet now pulled up against her chin.

'Now they'll all know,' she said.

'Well they are going to anyway. So he might as well tell them.'

'I'd better get to mother. If she gets to hear on the grapevine, through whispers in the corridors, she'll be devastated.'

Mary jumped up and reached for her underclothes that were strewn on the floor at the foot of the bed. She dressed quickly, pushing the buttons of her dress into their eyes as fast as she could. She retrieved her shoes, which had found their way over into one of the corners of the room, and then leant across the bed and gave him a goodbye kiss.

'Goodbye,' she said, breathlessly.

'See you in the morning then. Hope everything goes well with your mother.'

And with that she was gone. He lay there listening to her footsteps as she scurried away down the corridor towards the seamstress' room.

*****

Thinking back about it all several months later Eleanor considered that she had taken the news rather calmly.

It was certainly a great surprise to her. She really had no idea that her daughter had become so close to him. True she had heard one or two whispers, but she had simply dismissed them as idle gossip. On reflection she was naturally pleased. Pleased that Mary had found herself another partner. Pleased too that he was so wealthy and established. Sure, she ruminated, as she began to clear Mary's house, he was somewhat older than her and she knew that he had something of a reputation, but on balance Mary really had done rather well for herself.

They had made some progress clearing the house, but two months later there was still much she had left to finish. All day she packed items into tea chests. She was amazed at how much stuff Mary had accumulated in the two years that she had been living there. She wasn't the best at keeping house, she thought, but this was taking untidiness to an extreme. On reflection she was kinder, remembering that the last year had been especially difficult for Mary, and housework would, understandably, have not been important.

She shifted the second full tea chest towards the front door and slid an empty one to the far end of the room, where all the books were stacked. As she picked them out, handful by handful, a manila folder with a bow fell from the shelf and hit her foot. Gathering it up she was curious as to what it might contain, and so stepping over items still lying on the floor, she went and sat down in a chair near the window to take a break and find out. Untying the bow, opening the folder and seeing the writing there she realised at once that it was something belonging to Guy. She leafed through it casually, intrigued to see what he had written. On page after page were notes about meetings he had attended, Court hearings that he had sat through, and individuals whom he had interviewed. Towards the back she came across a drawing, which he had pasted on one of the pages. It was a romantic picture of two lovebirds in a cage with the words 'Love' written along the perch, on which they were both stood. She smiled and then let out a little chuckle of joy as she realised that Mary had drawn it for him. She continued to flick through the pages, now beginning to lose interest, when something on one of the pages caught her attention. She stopped and turned back to it and began to read the notes that he had scribbled there.

*****

John Mullay.

Family have lived in England for around five hundred years. On the estate since around that time.

Have been able to trace his family back through some of that time. Family altered name in 1600+ from De Molay.

Originally came from France.

Famous relative Jacques De Molay*. He was the twenty third Grand Master of the Knights Templar, the Crusaders, who took Jerusalem in the thirteen century.

The Knights Templar were considered to have riches and were seen as threatening the Catholic Church and so were rounded up on Friday 13 October 1307 in France on the instruction of Philip, King of France, and with the endorsement of Pope Clement.

The Knights Templar were imprisoned and tortured. Jacques De Molay was incarcerated for seven years until on 18 March 1314, when he was roasted slowly over a smokeless fire on an island in the Seine.

John Mullay has a Holy Bible, black, leather bound, which he keeps in his study and which he takes to church. Written in there is a list of names and dates. Heading this list are the words 13 October 1307. Underneath those words is written Deuteronomy 32:53. The text at that reference in the Holy Bible reads:

'To me belongeth vengeance and recompense; their foot shall slide in due time: for the day of their calamity is at hand, and the things that shall come upon them make haste.'

The list below contains eight names. Two are John Akehurst and Elizabeth Haines. Besides their names is the date 1826. On that list too is Matthew Royce and the date 1831. He was killed in Redhill on 13 October that year by criminals as yet unknown. JA and EH were also killed on 13 October.

My contention is that their murders have something to do with the Knights Templar. Perhaps a group of them still exists. It is also my contention that the leader of this group is John Mullay. These look like they might be revenge killings. All those murdered held the Catholic faith.

* Jacques De Molay is a non fictional character and the events relating to his death are true.

*****

Eleanor turned over the page but she was to be disappointed for there the notes ended. She quickly turned back the page and reread it, stopping to stare, through tearful eyes, at her father's name inscribed there.

She could feel the rage beginning to swell inside her as she realised what Guy had uncovered. She realised too that his own death might somehow be linked to this. Perhaps he hadn't been discrete enough. If that was the case someone had wanted him silenced and were organised and ruthless enough to execute him. She sat slumped in the chair, unable to move, the pain now so shockingly revisited. Memories came flooding back and the hurt that she experienced at that time was now just as vivid in her mind as it had been in reality then.

There was a knock on the door. Glancing across she caught sight of John Mullay stood outside. Her anger welled over. She made her way to the kitchen, taking a knife from the drawer, she then approached the door, and as she lifted the latch it opened. He gave her a curt acknowledgement before stepping into the house and walking passed her into the front room.

'Mary not here yet?' he asked, dismissively.

'No.'

'She won't be long I suppose. What are you up to? Clearing her stuff?'

'Yes.'

There was a long silence and then Eleanor, enraged, stepped forward and thrust the knife towards his face. He was quick enough to try and parry it, the blade slicing his right hand as he did so, before its point daggered deep into his neck. Blood began to pour and then gushed from the wound, as he sank to the floor. A pool of blood oozed, warm and crimson, settling in the hair at the back of his head. He gurgled, gasping for air. Eleanor stood above him. Shocked. Frightened. Panicked. She turned and ran to the door, leaving it open, as she ran down the road towards Bookham.

Mary had seen her mother running ungainly away from her. She called out but Eleanor hadn't seemed to hear her. Entering the house she could hear a moan, frightened and despairing, coming from the front room.

'Oh my God,' she screamed, as she saw him lying there.

Kneeling alongside him she tried to comfort him. He seemed to recognise her voice, but didn't turn his head, the blade still lodged in his throat preventing that. She stroked his forehead, now cold and damp, and could only watch as life left him. She stayed there for about five minutes, stroking his head, back and forward, back and forward, as the blood lying on the floor seeped into the fabric of her new dress.

*****

'Hello. Anyone there?'

The voice she heard was his personal aide's. She didn't reply. He stepped inside the house and having looked into the kitchen popped his head around the door of the front room.

'Dear God! Get away girl,' he shouted, as he stepped around her and knelt beside him. He could see that he was dead.

'Stay there Mary,' he instructed, firmly, 'I'll go back to the house to get help. Don't move anything. Understand?'

She stared up at him vacantly, still on her knees, her face pale.

'Understand?' he shouted.

She nodded.

'Good,' and he left at haste, running as fast as he could back to the house.

She crouched there until she began to feel her knees ache and her right leg begin to deaden with pins and needles. Standing to shake her leg to get some feeling into it, she caught sight of the folio, still open at the page on which Guy's notes were written. Bending over she picked them up and read the page. Then a page, loose in the folio, dropped and fluttered to the floor at her feet. Gathering it up she ran her eyes down it and saw Will's name there. Carefully she read and then reread the letter. Twice. The room reverberated with an anguished scream.

Her mind was in a rage of pain and hate as she got to her knees again and seizing the knife handle withdrew it from his throat. Grasping it firmly in both hands she plunged it deep into his chest. She felt a bone crack as she did so, and then a sound like a bagpipe winding up for play, as air released from his inners. As she lay there, the knife handle still grasped in her hands, her head sunk onto his stomach, the personal aide pulled up outside the house with a trap. He was accompanied by one of the grounds men.

His strong hands took her firmly by the shoulders and pulled her away.

'Move away Mary.'

She knelt there, impassive.

'Move her away Simon.'

The grounds man stepped alongside her and putting his hand under her armpit heaved her up and to one side. As she staggered to her feet she let out a scream and threw herself at his personal aide, her hands battering his chest. Grabbing her hands he spun her round and pushed her towards the door, as the grounds man took her around the waist and heaved her, kicking, through the front door.

Calmly the aide picked up the folio, and opening it where the loose page had created the mark, he glanced at Guy's text and then the letter itself. Without showing any emotion he tore the pages from the folio and together with the letter stuffed them into his jacket, and then tossed the remainder of the folio into one of the tea chests. Kneeling down above John Mullay he kissed him softly on his forehead and closed his eyes, which had stared blankly at him.

'Let's get Mary back to the house. Then can you take the trap into Bookham, Simon, and go and find the constable. You know where he lives?'

'Yes sir.'

'Right. Let's get her up.'

'Sir.'

Mary by now was subdued, her hysteria having passed. She felt limp and lifeless as she stood there, blood smeared over her hands and splattered across the front of her dress.

'Up you get.' He took her elbow as he helped her into the trap.

'I'll walk back up to the house, sir. There's not really enough room up there for the three of us.'

'No. You squeeze in Simon. We need to make sure Mary doesn't come to any harm.'

'Sir.'

Rounding the corner towards the front of the house they paid no attention to the incredulous stares that they received from two young chambermaids, who were walking down the drive. They watched the trap go passed them and turned to witness its passage to the front door, before carrying on, now deep in animated conversation.

'Let's get her up to his room.'

'Yes sir.'

Either side of her, each holding firmly an arm, hastily they walked Mary up the staircase.

'Right Mary, sit there,' the personal aide instructed her, pointing to a hard chair stood against a wall at the far end of the room.

She sat meekly, her shoulders slumped, her hands clasped together tightly on her lap, her expressionless face now drawn.

'Right Simon, you'd better be off. As quick as you can.'

'Yes sir.'

He stood above her, alone now. Her gaze fixed on the floorboards, she saw his black boots approach. She looked up at him, slowly.

'You stupid, stupid bitch,' he screamed, and then hit her hard across the side of her face with the back of his right hand.

Shaken she had to hold herself to stop herself sliding sideways off the seat. Her expression didn't change as she continued to just stare up at him. Turning away from her, she listened to his footsteps cross the room, the door slam shut and the key turn as he locked her inside.

His eyes scanned the shelves. At first he couldn't see it, Then at the far end, tucked in deep between two large volumes he sighted its black leather cover. Reaching up he drew it down and flicked the pages, back and forward until he came across the page he was looking for. He read the headings and his eyes cast down the list before him. The top of the page tore easily as he took great care as he edged the tear downwards. He felt for the papers from the folio that he had placed in his pocket and screwing them all tightly together threw them into the fire opposite. The flame shot, brighter than it had been, as the papers burned, their vanilla colour turning quickly to a flaky grey. He picked up a poker, which lay beside the grate, and scarified the flimsy embers to nothing.

*****

Constable Hall came to the house about two hours later. The personal aide introduced himself courteously and took him into an adjoining room off the main entrance. He explained, without being over dramatic, that there had been a murder that afternoon and that John Mullay was lying dead in a house alongside the driveway, where he had been slain by Mary Ayres, who was now being held in a locked room on the first floor. The constable was impressed by the man's dignified calmness, and took notes, verbatim, as he spoke. The aide paused whenever he sensed that the constable was having difficulty keeping up with the pace.

'You say John Mullay is in a house just down the drive?'

'Yes.'

'Why would he have been there?'

'The house has been lived in by Mary Ayres since she got married here on the estate. She continued to live in the house after her husband, Guy Soden, died last year.'

'Ah, yes. Guy Soden. Of course. Tragic.'

He forgot about the question he had just asked as he recalled the events and the horror he had experienced seeing the decomposed remains of the man when they had retrieved him from the well the previous summer.

'Well if you could take me there that would be a good start.'

'Certainly. Perhaps we can take your trap down there? It'll save you time.'

The house was beginning to darken as they entered it but the light was more than sufficient for the constable to see for himself the carnage before him. It was evident that the man had been brutally murdered and that the evidence, the slashed throat and the knife protruding stiffly from his chest, supported the tale of events, which had been described so diligently by the aide. He surveyed the scene, made several notes in his book, before turning to the aide.

'Very sad. Very sad indeed. So Mary Ayres is locked in the house you say?'

'Yes.'

'Well I would ask that you keep her there. I'll need to get to Union Hall before dark and plan to be back early tomorrow, around eight most likely, with colleagues. You'll need to lock this house up and leave everything as it is now. We shall remove his body to Union Hall in the morning and take Mary Ayres there too at that time.'

'Understood, constable.'

They secured the house and then the constable turning to the personal aide said

'Good. Shall I take you back to the house?'

He declined the offer saying that he needed the air and would prefer to walk.

'Its only a five minute walk. Thank you for the offer though.'

'No trouble. Well then, until tomorrow.'

*****

Mary left the broth that had been brought to her the previous evening by the aide. He had found her still sat motionless in the chair where he had left her. She didn't speak to him, neither had she responded when he advised her that the police would be here to collect her in the morning. Once he had locked her in for the night she had got up and wandered around the room, staring out through the large windows that she loved into the dark, seeing nothing other than her shadow flickering in the light of the lit candle that he had left her. Eventually she lay on the bed, only venturing under the covers when she awoke in the middle of the night, ice cold.

The turn of carriage wheels on the gravel outside had woken her around eight as she lay there forlorn and sad. And then footsteps approaching alerted her and she hastily clambered down from the four poster, trying to straighten the bedding, as they unlocked the door. She felt unclean and her mouth tasted acidy.

Two men, strong and tall stood behind the constable as he stepped forward, his right hand extended towards her.

'Mary Ayres, I'd like you to come with me now,' he said, in a matter of fact sort of way.

Nodding, she collected up her skirt, which had got tangled up with some bedding, and as she did so she noted really for the first time the blood, dry and stained on both her hands, and the smeared red stains across her chest and along the hemline of her clothing. Constable Hall was immediately aware of the shocked look that she gave on seeing that.

'Come now, Mary,' he said more gently, as she rounded the bed and stood there passively in front of him.

238

The two men stepped forward and one of them clasped her hands in his, tightly, making her wince, as the second man manacled her wrists firm.

'Take her to the wagon,' he commanded, and they hauled her at pace from the room and down the staircase.

'Inside you get,' one of them shouted, unnecessarily, as the other held open the door into the wagon. She stepped up, he unceremoniously pushing her up and forward with a large hand stuffed hard against her bottom. The second man clambered inside after her and began to tie her manacled hands to the side of the wagon with a metal chain. Once he had done that he jumped out and slammed the door shut. She sat motionless in the darkness as he bolted the door tight shut. Seconds later her whole body began to shake. A mixture of pure fear and deep grief.

—◊—

Seventeen

His piercing blue eyes surveyed her from across the room. He stood motionless and still as if watching a prey. She looked at him. His expressionless face seemed to her quite gentle, but his demeanour and manner betrayed that sentiment. She dropped her gaze and sat, unsteady and very unsure, her hands clasped tight on her lap. The silence was only broken by the heavy nasal wheezing of one of the guards stood behind her at the door. He sneezed and she jumped. Her reaction made her smile.

'What's there to smile about?'

The harshness of his voice frightened her. She looked up at him again and now saw for herself the fierce temperament that lurked, shallow, beneath.

'Well?'

'Nothing,' she ventured limply.

'No. Nothing.' He took a step forward, inhaled heavily, and then spat out the single word

'Why?'

She didn't respond immediately, not sure really what he had meant.

'Why what?' she responded hesitatingly, scared that she might incur his anger once again.

'Why did you kill him?'

'Oh.'

'Yes. Oh.'

He took a step nearer her and stood just in front of where she sat. His toes in his black, highly polished leather boots now only inches away from her own tiny feet. She felt a tremble run along her spine and a small bead of sweat appear in the small of her back.

'I felt enraged. He sent my friend Will away to the Caribbean and he 's now dead. And he murdered my grandfather and his partner.'

'Who's Will?'

'Will. He is. No was. No, is a friend of mine. We lived together, sort of, several years ago. He was sent away. Transported. To his plantation. As a slave.'

'As a slave? As a slave?' he said for the second time, more slowly, sneering at her assertion.

'Yes.'

'And who is your grandfather?'

John Akehurst. He lived in Bookham. He was killed on 13 October 1826 because he was a Catholic.'

'Really? You do live an interesting life.' He spat out the words, the sarcasm in his voice penetrating her instantly.

'It's true,' she pleaded. Her words sounded pitiful as she spoke them, and she knew it. She dropped her head again and stared at her fingers held tight together by the irons.

'And why did you feel you needed to stab him in the chest once you had slashed his throat?'

She didn't answer. Her mind rewound through the events. Vividly she could once again see her mother fleeing. 'Dear Lord' she thought, 'I can't involve her.'

'I wanted to punish him.'

'You wanted to punish him?' he said, deliberately and slowly.

'Now tell me. What was your relationship with him?'

'I worked for him.'

'Yes. I know that much. But I'm told that you were more than that to him.'

She hesitated at first, and then responded as assertively as she was able,

'Yes, we were good friends too.'

'Good friends,' he repeated, and as he did so he stepped behind her.

She felt his head come down next to hers. He whispered

'You were lovers?'

'Yes,' she said, almost inaudibly.

'So why would you want to kill your lover? A rich benefactor?'

She turned her head slightly and her eyes met his, more tired and dark looking now.

'Because he killed my grandfather and harmed my Will.'

He stood up and paced across the room, turning sharply on his heels.

'So you said,' he shouted. 'Now let's just get one thing signed off here. I'm getting tired of hearing your fantasies. You killed him. You admit that much?'

There was a long silence in the room as she deliberated over that statement. He stood, taut, his arms now crossed, staring through her.

'Well?' he shouted, once her silence had become too much for him.

'Yes. I killed him.'

'Well at least we know that as a fact. Get a pen and paper,' he demanded to one of the guards.

When the guard returned they brought in a small table and placed it in front of her. The paper and pen, which lay on the table askew, were straightened and brought closer to her by the interrogator.

'Write,' he demanded.

She couldn't stop her hands shaking as she penned the words, which he spoke aloud for her to copy

'I, Mary Ayres, confess that I did murder John Mullay at my house on his estate on 18 November 1834.'

'Sign.'

She scrawled her signature and then placed the pen neatly alongside the document.

He picked it up off the desk and blew it to dry the ink, which had run off the pen at several points as she had written and even now were forming small pools.

'Take her to Guildford,' he ordered, as he stepped out of the room and strode off down the corridor.

*****

The doctor examining her on arrival at Guildford prison looked at her naked body with curiosity. He couldn't but help notice her navel. Hard and full.

'You're pregnant my girl,' he said, sounding pleased and excited, forgetting for a second where he was.

'Pregnant?'

'Yes, young lady. Three months I would guess. I'll inform the governor's office so they look after you properly in your condition.'

She ran her hands over her stomach and realised as she did so that she hadn't been herself lately. So that was it she thought, a broad smile crossing her face.

'You look pleased.'

'I am. I really am.'

*****

The aide read the notice posted outside the Court House. The trial date was stated; two months hence. He noted that the Judge would hear the case. He smiled and turned to return to his carriage stood in the side street opposite. Sitting with his valise on his lap inside the carriage he penned a letter to the Judge requesting a meeting to review his investment in the Caribbean. He watched as the softened wax hardened slowly on the envelope and felt a sense of pride as he read the motif on his seal. 'Fortis et Fidelis'. He certainly had that for sure, and as he thought it, he smiled. Once the wax had hardened he called the driver and requested him to deliver the missive that afternoon, after they had returned to the estate.

They met two days later. The Judge had watched as the carriage made its way towards him. He heard the butler greet the man and ask him to wait in the hall.

'Show him in,' he said, before the man could speak.

'Sir.'

'How good it is to meet you again,' the personal aide effervesced, ignoring the fact that at their last meeting he had been but a silent witness.

'Yes. How nice.'

The aide, now seated where his master had been seated at the earlier meeting, exchanged a few pleasantries, before the Judge, getting a little tired of them and feeling that his status was being somewhat usurped in his own home, interrupted, impolitely.

'Well, what would you like to speak to me about?'

'Yes,' he said for time, gathering his thoughts, aware that he had probably been a little too effusive. 'I wanted to assure you that even though John Mullay has sadly passed away that your investment in his project is secure and will remain so for the duration of the loan period. I am now responsible for overseeing the plantation and can assure you that it thrives. There is something that I should like to offer you in exchange for an additional increase in the return on your investment.'

'Yes?'

The personal aide noted the man's eager reaction that he had witnessed before. The man was fired by greed he reflected, then he continued:

'The trial of the girl who murdered John Mullay is to be heard by you in a month. No doubt she will hang.'

However, as he continued his words were drowned out by the sound of something falling heavily in the adjacent hall. The butler stepped into the room, and serenely apologised for the commotion and informed the Judge that a chandelier had fallen and would he take great care.

'Quite so,' he said, without hesitating, and turned back to the aide, whose audacious proposition he had heard despite the din. The Judge eyed him, his face slightly contorted as he screwed his eyes to shield them from the light that now streamed through the window across his face. It unsettled the aide and he shifted in his seat. The Judge said nothing, rose and wandered across to the mahogany desk in the corner of the room. He shifted a few papers lying on the desk and leant across and picked one of them up. He read its contents carefully to himself.

'Next month you say?'

'Yes.'

'Yes, you're right. Mary Ayres. Murder. Pregnant too. Did she do it?'

'Certainly. I understand that the police have a signed confession.'

'Really?' he paused. 'Well in that case,' and he walked slowly back and sat down, heavily, into the back of his chair. 'What are you offering if I do what you ask?'

Another five percent, annually and ten percent of the plantation when the loan is repaid.'

'Twenty percent, today.'

The aide pondered, deliberately, his mind pleased that the Judge had been as consistent as he had remembered.

'Fine. That's settled then.'

He had expected the Judge to call for drinks as he had done before. He was to be somewhat disappointed when the Judge rose, and with no sign of exuberance or positive emotion said:

'Well, I suppose you'll want to be getting on your way then?'

'Yes, I suppose I will. Thank you.'

The butler appeared at the door.

'My guest is leaving.'

'Sir.'

'Goodbye,' he said without feeling, and as he spoke he just turned and returned to his mahogany desk.

—⟋⟍—

Eighteen

She felt that she was coping quite well with prison life. It was fair to say that in her condition it seemed that particular attention was being given to her. She appreciated that. Others did not have it so easy. The cells she passed on her way to and from the doctor were always full and the stench emanating from them she still had not yet learnt to ignore. She covered her nose with her hand every time and held her breath as long as she could until she came again into fresher air. Each cell had at least thirty incarcerated in it. There was barely room to lie down. Those stood at the bars held out their hands as much for the comforting touch of a gentle human contact as much as for food. She had just the once gone to touch someone. Never again would she do that. Her hand had almost been wrenched from her wrist as the prisoner, who had grasped her, pulled and then manically sunk her teeth deep into the fleshiest part of her forearm. Fortunately another inmate, seeing her distress, had ripped the maniac off her. The bleeding didn't stop for at least an hour and each time she had looked at her arm since the scar reminded her to take great care.

The cell she had was cramped. There was room for just three at a push. On the south side of the prison with a tiny window, covered with a metal mesh, high up on one wall, she and her two cellmates at least got some light and fresh air. She had liked Annette from the moment they first met and they had become relaxed friends during the month she had been there. Ruth joined them a few days later and she too seemed pleasant and easy going at first, but had become increasingly domineering each day. She was never particularly unpleasant, but her manner and put downs began to grind Mary down. She decided soon after she had arrived that she would keep her distance. That was a little more difficult to do in such a confined space than she had anticipated, but she accepted the challenge and found it gave her something other her upcoming trial to think about each day.

The relationship between Annette and Ruth seemed to blossom daily and soon the two of them were always close, laughing and joking with each other. By the second week it had become obvious that the two of them were sleeping together and Mary had to suffer most nights listening in the pitch dark to their intimate playfulness. Distracted at first she soon came to see it as something rather kind and gentle in an otherwise harsh environment. She began to miss Guy as never before, and she thought deeply and even more fondly of Will than she had always done since their first meeting so many years ago.

They had little to do during the day and so amused themselves making up bits of stories, which the other had then to embellish, before handing on to the next storyteller. When they played that game they invariably all ended up in a heap, tears streaming down their cheeks as they writhed in mirth.

Most of the time they just sat. Impassive. Looking up at the changing colours flitting across the window, which sometimes were reflected on a wall opposite. Other times they just watched as inmates passed their cell on their way to or from Court.

There was always something to listen to for the prison was for much of its twenty four hours alive with a variety of noises, which once registered in your memory informed you of the time or the event taking place out of your sight. Strangely, Mary found that time passed quickly.

Her trial date duly arrived and she was readied for presentation to the Court. Her hair was cut. She was bathed and disinfected. Her clothes were changed. On the morning of her trial as she stood in the cold yard watching the wagon move towards her, she looked and felt pristine. Her condition by now was very evident and as she moved around she found that it was beginning to be a little uncomfortable. They kindly helped her up into the wagon before more gently than she had experienced in the past locked her manacled hands to a pillar in the centre of the vehicle. She was alone for the first time in several months and the experience, frightening at first, she soon found exhilarating. She was beginning, almost, to enjoy such a freedom when the wagon turned into the Court House and descended into its deep basement, stopped, and the door was swung open, revealing to her the reality of two burly guards waiting to take her inside.

Held in a cold cell for most of the day, she was visited just the once by her defence lawyer, whom she had first met in Guildford three weeks earlier. He had been very professional in his dealings with her but made it clear that the best that she might expect would be to get a long sentence as a result of her current condition. He said they called it 'pleading the belly'. That had made her laugh and he was glad that he had been able to cheer her in such uncivil surroundings.

'Well that's what we'll do,' she had said to him confidently that day, and she repeated the same sentiment to him again when they met at the Court House.

'You will be pleading guilty?' he had asked her for confirmation.

She hesitated, had a flash thought about her mother, whom she had not seen or spoken to since that day, and then replied nonchalantly,

'Of course.'

'Good. It really is the only way a plea for clemency might be well received. It usually is. Good luck.'

She watched as he moved to the door, banged on it to be released, and then strode off towards the Court.

The cell door closed she went and sat quietly on the wooden bench in the corner. She began to bite her fingernails. The first time she had done that since she was six years old.

*****

They put her in a new cell when she returned to Guildford Prison. She wasn't alone. Her new cell

companion was about the same age as her and had
been there for two months awaiting trial. It was alleged
that she had murdered her father. She denied it, of
course, and kept repeating her denial regularly to
Mary. Mary by contrast tried not to dwell on her
situation. She had learned very quickly since being in
prison to take each day as it came and only to think
of this place as your entire existence. What had been
has existed and cannot now be revisited, and what
was to come did not yet exist and must be expected,
impassively. It seemed to work for her.

The two of them got on quite well. Their little cell was set
apart from the central section of the prison and so was
for the most part much quieter. The warders even seemed
gentler Mary thought, or possibly she was becoming all
too familiar and comfortable with her surroundings.
They passed the time in a routine that accidentally they
had set for themselves. Each morning they would both
clean the cell, getting down on their hands and knees and
scrubbing with strips of cloth that they had been given by
one of the guards. Her cell mate seemed to take particular
pride in spotlessness, and would often redo bits of the cell
that were perfectly clean and which she had only just
done an hour earlier. Mary watched her incredulously
at first, passing critical comment. She soon came to
understand that that was part of the girl's make up and
probably part of her problem. So now she simply took to
her wooden bunk at the far end of the cell and watched
her with quiet amusement.

They would share the food that came to their cell around
midday, and would eat it together, sat side by side on

Mary's bunk. They were not given any utensils and so picked lumps of food out of the tin pot with their fingers, and gently poured the liquids straight down their throats. The food was just about edible, although it was always hugely greasy and best eaten fast, while still tepid, before the fat congealed into a skin on the top. Then it was unbearably foul both to look at, to think about, and most of all to taste.

They developed a number of games to amuse themselves during the remainder of the afternoon. One which Mary liked in particular was the one in which each told three or four lines of a story and then passed it over to the other to carry on with the tale. She had played that one before and it always led to howls of laughter. With this girl it just was not the same, and so much of the time they played a more childish game such as 'I Spy'. As the cell was limited in what it offered as objects, that was, understandably, restrictive. It didn't seem to matter to the girl. She was happy to play the game for hour after hour, every day. Day after day the same objects appeared in the game, until Mary had to feign ignorance in order to prolong the whole thing. She was now beginning to understand the girl with whom she was sharing the cell. She reminded her more and more of a little girl at school, whom they had all been horrible to so many years ago. Cottonhead they had nicknamed her.

As the months passed Mary grew fuller. She could now feel the baby inside her. She was taken weekly to see the doctor and he seemed pleased with her progress. The birth was due at the end of May, a little over a month away now. They showed her the room where she would have the baby. It was a small almost empty room just off the doctor's surgery. There was a bed there and little else. Once, when she was visiting the surgery and being attended to by one of the nurses, she could hear one of the other girls having their baby next door. It sounded awful she thought to herself. The sound of the baby's cry had raced through her and brought her to tears of joy.

'There, there,' the nurse had said, 'isn't it just wonderful. That'll be you very soon.'

She sobbed all the way back to the cell. Confused at what she was actually thinking. Unable to control her emotions. That evening she lay quietly, hour after hour, on her bunk. Silent. Her cell mate sat on the floor next to her stroking her hair softly, trying, without any sign of success, to comfort her.

Days passed. They had resumed their routine. Now, however, Mary did not move much from her bunk and certainly didn't clean as before. She simply lay there much of the time, heavy, pointing to spots of dirt for her cell mate to clean. She enjoyed the fun of that.

Then one day the pain became unbearable. She screamed. They came quickly. Seeing her condition she was taken immediately to the surgery. Her labour did not last long. Within two hours she had given birth and could hear the child crying in the adjoining room. She lay there, moist and tired, waiting for them to return with a bundled child for her to coddle. Then it became silent. She waited. It must have been an hour before someone came and spoke to her again.

'Well Mary, you can go back down to your cell now.'

'Where's the baby?'

'Come on Mary. Up you get,' she said, as she grabbed her arm to lever her upwards and off the bed.

'Where's the baby?' she said again, but this time more insistently.

The doctor hearing the commotion came through into the room. He looked aggravated. Whereas he had been gentle and kind to her, now he simply grabbed her arm and said harshly:

'Now don't fuss Mary. No fuss. Let's get you back to your cell.'

'Where's the baby?'

He stared at her and spat out his words:

'The baby has gone Mary. It's gone to its new home. You must simply forget all about this time.'

She looked disbelievingly at him. Her face crumpled and then pain such as she had never ever experienced before seized her mind. She tried to resist their clawing hands at first. Then, finally, she felt her spirit break, and lay limply as they dragged her off the bed and back to her cell.

*****

That day there was great joy on the estate. The wet nurse waited expectantly as she watched their arrival.

The aide beamed as he stepped down from the carriage, the babe now wrapped in a fine silk dress and bonnet lay asleep oblivious to his surroundings, and the beginnings of a privileged life.

*****

She was allowed visitors on the Thursday they said. She sat in the cell alone now and hadn't expected anyone to come.

'Someone to see you here Mary,' the guard spoke, caringly, as he opened the door wide.

Mary looked up, listlessly, and then surprised at seeing her, she leapt to her feet and threw her arms around her neck, kissing her fiercely up and down her nape.

'Mother. Oh, mother,' she kept repeating. 'You came. You came.'

They stood clutching each other for some time, not wanting to break the moment.

'You look well,' she said, as she pushed Mary to arms length, holding her shoulders in her hands and looking deep into her eyes.

'I'm fine.' There was a long pause as she hesitated to consider the next sentence in her head

'It's such a long time since I last saw you. You were in such a hurry. Didn't you hear me calling you?'

Her mother ignored the question.

'It is such a long time. I'm so sorry I couldn't be in Court to give you support dear. I've been very ill.'

'I understand. How are you anyway? You look thinner than I remember.'

'I'm fine now. Just some stomach troubles, which I've got over.'

'How's the village?'

'Uh,' she exclaimed. 'Haven't been there for a while now. When I was released from work on the estate and you were here people just shunned me. I couldn't believe it at first. But there you are. That's friends, so called, for you. I've been staying with a real friend near Horsham since the end of last year.'

'No? Are you working now?

'No.'

'Oh.'

They stood looking at each other, not sure what to say, hesitant to talk about anything that might be upsetting. The guard, who had stood motionless in the doorway, stepped into the corridor, half closing the door behind him.

'Let's sit down,' Mary said taking her mother's hand and walking her over to the wooden bench. 'Sorry about the toilet,' she laughed as she pointed towards the hole close by.

'No matter dear.'

Holding hands tenderly, Mary rubbing her thumb softly along the line of her mother's knuckle, they sat together in silence for a little while.

'He killed grandfather didn't he,' she ventured, haltingly and in a whisper, after the silence had become a little too uncomfortable for her.

'Yes, he did.'

'I saw you running away you know.'

'Did you?'

'Yes. I was so shocked when I saw him lying there. He died in my arms. You know that I loved him then?'

'Yes. You did. I know. I was so pleased for you. But...'

'He had Will sent away. You know that don't you?'

'Really?' she answered, shocked and disbelieving.

'He's dead now. And Guy. Poor, poor Guy. He must have known too much.'

Silence.

'I'm so sorry Mary. It should be me. I was so scared.'

'No,' and as she spoke she leant forward and clutched her mother, 'No. Never.'

They sat; clasped; as one; like they had never been before.

'Time.'

The word shattered their union, and they both sat up, separate again.

She looked helplessly at her daughter. Her face now as sad and as desperate as she had ever seen it.

Lost for words to say she once more gripped her hands, kissed her forehead. Lingering, to feel the delicate skin for the last time.

'God bless you, darling. God bless you.'

'Mother,' she screeched. Desperate now, the tone of her voice vivid evidence of her deep anguish.

She felt her mother's hand slip, slowly, from her and watched as she fled the room, weeping.

—⁓—

Nineteen

Tall and stiff he stood on the edge of the wooden boards watching the cart approach. The crowd were unusually silent as the frail girl was brought down and led to the steps. She seemed calm enough he thought. Two men held her elbows as they pulled her up the stairs and led her towards him. The priest had followed them up the flight and now stood to one side. The text he recited floated away, unheard for the most part as the crowd edged nearer and became noisier. He stepped towards her, his face hidden from her view by the leather mask. She saw his eyes, and saw anxiety there. He saw in hers fear.

From his belt he pulled a black linen cover and in one motion placed it over her head. He pushed her, gently at first, and then suddenly more firmly towards the rope that hung just above. Pulling it he placed it around her neck, quickly. And then as he stepped back he kicked the pin away with his right foot.

The crowd roared their approval as she hung. Stiff at first; and then limp.

Her last thought in the blackness had been that she had lived life well and had been loved.

The End

Lightning Source UK Ltd.
Milton Keynes UK
29 December 2010

164962UK00001B/34/P